Slave to Grace

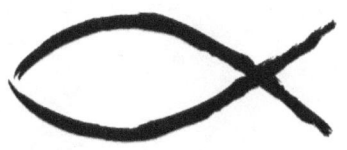

DocUmeant *Publishing*
85 N. Main Street
Florida, NY 10921
646-233-4366

Disclaimer: All characters except those named in the book of Philemon have been named after authentic Christian martyrs listed either in Foxe's Book of Martyr's or other martyr lists.

Scripture quotations are taken from the Holy Bible, New Living Translation, copyright ©1996, 2004, 2007 by Tyndale House Foundation. Used by permission of Tyndale House Publishers, Inc., Carol Stream, Illinois 60188. All rights reserved.

Ginger Marks Cover design and Layout
DocUmeantDesigns, www.DocUmeantDesigns.com

Philip S Marks Editor

Distributed by DocUmeant Publishing
For inquiries about volume orders, please contact:
DocUmeant Publishing
publisher@documeantpublishing.com

Second Edition

Printed in the United States Of America
ISBN-13: 978-1-937801-34-2 (paperback)
ISBN-10: 1937801349

Slave to Grace

FREEDOM COMES IN UNEXPECTED WAYS

JOYCE FOX

DocUmeant *Publishing*
85 N Main St
Florida NY 100921
646-233-4366
www.DocUmeantPublishing.com

DEDICATION

To my dearest Art who "always protects, always trusts, always hopes, always perseveres." I Cor. 13:7

PREFACE

This letter is from Paulus, in prison for preaching the Good News about Christ Jesus, and from our brother Timothy. It is written to Philemon, our much loved co-worker, and to our sister Apphia and to Archippus, a fellow soldier of the cross. I am also writing to the church that meets in your house.

May God our Father and the Lord Jesus Christ give you grace and peace.

I always thank God when I pray for you, Philemon, because I keep hearing of your trust in the Lord Jesus and your love for all of God's people. You are generous because of your faith. And I am praying that you will really put your generosity to work, for in so doing you will come to an understanding of all the good things we can do for Christ. I myself have gained much joy and comfort from your love, my brother, because your kindness has so often refreshed the hearts of God's people. That is I am boldly asking a favor of you. I could demand it in the name of Christ because it is the right thing for you to do, but because of our love, I prefer just to ask you. So take this as a request from your friend Paul, an old man, now in prison for the sake of Christ Jesus.

My plea is that you show kindness to Onesimus. I think of him as my own son because he became a believer as a result of my ministry here in prison. Onesimus hasn't been of much use to you in the past, but now he is very useful to both of us. I am sending him back to you, and with him comes my own heart. I really wanted to keep him here with me while I am in these chains for preaching the Good News, and he would have helped me on your behalf. But I didn't want to do anything without your consent. And I didn't want you to help because you were forced to do it but because you wanted to.

Perhaps you could think of it this way: Onesimus ran away for a little while so you could have him back forever. He is no longer just a slave; he is a beloved brother, especially to me. Now he will mean much more to you, both as a slave and as a brother in the Lord. So if you consider me your partner, give him the same welcome you would give me if I were coming.

If he has harmed you in any way or stolen anything from you, charge me for it.

I, Paul, write this in my own handwriting: "I will repay it."

And I won't mention that you owe me your very soul! Yes, dear brother, please do me this favor for the Lord's sake. Give me this encouragement in Christ. I am confident as I write this letter that you will do what I ask and even more! Please keep a guest room ready for me, for I am hoping that God will answer your prayers and let me return to you soon. Epaphras, my fellow prisoner in Christ Jesus, sends you his greetings. So do Mark, Aristarchus, Demas, and Luke, my co-workers. The grace of the Lord Jesus Christ be with your spirit.

Acknowledgments

In honor of all those who have died for the faith of Jesus Christ.

CHAPTER ONE

Three Years Earlier

S old!" the slaver shouted. "You have bought yourself a fine slave, sir! One who is guaranteed to live up to his name. Not only is he a fine physical specimen, fit for heavy labor, he is educated and aristocratic in bearing, making him a candidate for the more cerebral tasks such as accounting and management work."

Philemon, who at six feet tall towered over his neighbors, gently took hold of his new property by the upper arm and began to lead him away through the crowd as he spoke to the seller. "Yes, yes. I know. If I'm not mistaken I've already told you I'll take him. Why *do* you continue to prattle on?" These slavers were about as trustworthy as rotted rope, but then what was one to do when one needed a new assistant?

"What did he mean, you'll live up to your name . . . . what *is* your name?" he inquired in a loud but kindly voice.

"Sir, he meant 'useful'. My name is Useful—Onesimus," came the quiet answer.

Onesimus paid no attention to his surroundings. He'd been raised in the city and the noises and smells and colors had no meaning for him. Philemon, on the other hand, spent time in the city for business purposes but lived in the country. The woman of obvious profession dressed in gold coins and red gauze raised no interest in him, but she was a distraction to be sure.

Philemon laughed as he sidestepped a pile of manure in the street, "Well, there's no reason to change your name! It sounds as if your father wanted to make you sale-able from your birth, Onesimus! Do you think that is a possibility?"

Wincing slightly at the admission, Onesimus nodded.

"Yes, sir. He may very well have. I have an older brother named Protos—Preeminent one—on whom he placed his hopes for his future well-being. While I was given the same training, he looked on me as something of a . . . replacement part. As if my brother was the chariot and I was the extra axle, should the original one crack." It was obvious the Useful One was hurt by this betrayal by his father and brother and his tone of voice made it clear that bitterness was spreading its ugly branches in his soul.

Philemon's face sobered as this piece of personal history was revealed. His heart ached at the pain Onesimus had unwittingly disclosed. He began to take note of the reed-slender, quiet young man. Approximately 5'8" tall, Onesimus was the same height as most of his contemporaries. He was also muscular for his frame, although he was wirier than most, lending an air of vulnerability that was further enhanced by his quiet manner. His deep-set brown eyes looked out of a face pock-marked, but not overly so, and his pale skin bespoke a youth of relative ease.

Philemon snagged a loaf of warm bread from a street vendor, tossing a coin to the woman. He ripped the loaf in two and offered half to Onesimus.

"And then your father... what? How did he come to the point where he had to offer his own son for sale?" Philemon asked quietly.

The newly-minted slave had to swallow hard to delay tearing into the first meal he'd had this day, but he manfully resisted the temptation and replied, "Father was never very good at handling money. He was a genius when it came to using his wealth to influence others, but he forgot to count the costs of his lavish gifts and parties I'm afraid." Ravenous, Onesimus could wait no more. He bit off a large bite of bread, chewed and swallowed rapidly, so he could continue his tale. "After years of counting as friends those who only liked him for his gifts, he found he had not only lost the family fortune but had also gotten himself into appalling debt. Lost in a bottomless pit of obligation to unscrupulous creditors, who would not hesitate to take what they felt was rightfully theirs, he had no choice... except the choice between the Pre-eminent one and the Useful one," Onesimus shrugged. "So, there really was no choice."

The two men walked on in silence as Philemon considered this information. "Well, Useful One," Philemon finally spoke, "have no fear. Your place will be keeping my accounts. As long as you can keep my records straight and my business on track, you needn't worry about spending your days in the fields beating olive trees!"

Onesimus' head of shiny black curls bobbed in agreement. "Sir, I've no doubt that I can be of great service to you in that regard. I've been trained from the age of five to write and figure and have much to offer in the line of transaction recording."

Reaching his litter, Philemon seated himself and motioned for Onesimus to walk along beside him as the bearers lifted the litter and made their way through the teeming streets of Colossae.

Their journey led them from the slave market, across the city, away from the chaotic noise emanating from smithies and children and fighting drunks, through streets of peaceful homes and streets of high commerce, far from the slave market and on out into the countryside north of town.

"These are my groves," Philemon revealed to his new acquisition as they passed acre after acre of gray and twisted olive trees. "It takes many workers to gather in the harvest and it is soon coming up. You will be kept busy enough tracking and keeping accurate records of the harvest. But your task shouldn't be too arduous, since I've been using a splendid accounting system for years. It shouldn't take you more than a couple of days to understand and learn how to use it."

Onesimus followed along as the litter was carried up a rise and through a small copse of shade trees. As they emerged from the trees, Onesimus was stunned by the magnificent view before him. In a grassy meadow where goats and sheep grazed, stood a great white and gleaming house and several large outbuildings that seemed to sparkle in the sunlight. Behind the buildings stretched an enormous vegetable garden. As the grass waved in the breeze it seemed to welcome its master home.

The litter pulled up before the front entrance of the house and was lowered to the ground as Philemon stepped from it to the earthen path beside it.

"Beautiful, isn't it?" He asked with obvious pride.

Onesimus could only nod in wonder.

"Justin!" Philemon shouted. "Justin, come here and show Onesimus to his quarters and then bring him to me in the pressing house."

To Onesimus, he continued, "Go with Justin. He is our chief houseman. Later, I will show you the pressing house."

Justin was a short, round man with a fringe of snowy hair surrounding his domed head and a bustling air both in his movements and his speech. He led the newcomer to a large building behind the main house. It, too, was dazzlingly white.

"This is where all the male house slaves are quartered except those who are married... oh, yes," he continued at the new arrival's raised eyebrows. "The master never breaks up a family. Should you find one of the female slaves attractive enough to wed, be assured the master will not stand in your way... but also be assured, he will not tolerate idle dalliance with the women. This is a Christian household and all must abide, even if we do not all believe," Justin prated as he led Onesimus into the building.

A row of old couches, comfortable still, but obviously replaced by newer for ones for the main household, lined one wall of the building. Between each couch and its neighbor stood an ample cupboard for housing clothing and other personal items. Each cupboard stood perpendicular to the wall so that each provided a modicum of privacy for the occupant of the couch it faced.

At the center of the room, another room arranged in similar fashion but with more couches and cupboards than the area they stood in, formed the elongated cross piece of a t-shape.

"The field workers sleep there," Justin said. "Not because of a class difference, but because they work on a different schedule. That way we do not disturb their rest times and they do not disturb ours," he explained.

Across from the couches were several tables upon which rested ewers and basins.

"Never appear before the master dusty or smelling," Justin continued. "He cannot abide untidiness."

"We eat our morning and evening meals here, at that table. At midday we sup in the cookhouse of the main house. Fine food it is, too. The same as the master eats. Even the field slaves feast on the same food, although they take their midday repast in the field."

Onesimus noticed that most of the ten couches in the Ts crosspiece, where they were standing, were obviously already occupied. There were two, though, that had no clothing in the adjoining cupboards and no bedclothes in evidence.

"You may have your choice of the two empty couches," his guide said warmly. Then he placed his hand on Onesimus' arm and leaned in to whisper with a conspiratorial grin, "Only, I wouldn't choose the one at the far end of the room. It stands next to Vitus' bed. Vitus is the scullery boy and he, sometimes . . . has a foot problem."

Onesimus smiled and wisely chose to take Justin's advice. He selected the fourth bed from the door and placed his small bundle upon the couch.

"Good enough for now!" declared Justin. "Let's not keep the master waiting any longer!"

Justin led him back out the door and up a winding side path to a large wooden building that stood on the southern edge of the compound beside the olive grove. Like all the buildings on the grounds, this building was lustrous, but it seemed to have no windows at all.

Onesimus' heart sank at the thought of spending his days cooped up in a black-dark building with no light but for the light of oil lamps. "It must be dark in there!" he murmured to Justin.

Justin walked to the door and gave a perfunctory knock. "Not at all. You'll understand in just a little bit," he commented as he cracked the door.

"Sir," he said, "Onesimus is settled in and is awaiting your instructions." Then he backed out and went back to his own duties.

As Onesimus started to reach out to open the door, the master slipped quickly past him and gave a shout. A small boy who carried two trussed and squawking chickens around his neck and a basket of bread, grapes, oil, and olives in his hands was moving rapidly across the lawn toward the road. Onesimus prepared to run after the boy who had obviously stolen the food and was now absconding with it. Just as he was about to give chase, the words Philemon was shouting became clear.

"AYE! Metra! Now you be careful with that basket. Don't spill it. And tell your mother there is plenty more when she needs it!"

Onesimus jumped as he felt something like a rock crash down on his left shoulder, but he quickly realized it was only the master's hand.

"Well and well. I daresay you thought he was filching, did you not?" he asked with a glint of humor in his eye. "You'll see in time that we help a lot of people around here when they are having difficulties; especially widows and children. I believe that's what the great God of Israel and His Son, Yeshua, would have us do in these difficult times."

Onesimus only nodded. He had little idea who "the great God of Israel and His Son, Yeshua" were, but he knew that simply declaring faith in those personages implied a repudiation of all the gods of Rome and that was a very dangerous path to take.

"With your permission, sir, I would ask you...," he hesitated.

At Philemon's lift of the eyebrows, he continued, "Are you claiming this God of Israel and His Son, Yeshua to be the deities you worship?"

The master chuckled. "You might say that, although they are only one deity. But never mind that just now. You will hear more tomorrow Lord's Day."

Onesimus felt his stomach flip over. Was this a god like the two-faced Janus of the Romans? Or was He a set of twins something like the founders of Rome, Romulus and Remus? He wasn't sure, but he knew he wanted nothing to do with this strange religion that declared two people to be one god!

"All the household comes every Lord's Day. The meeting is held right here, and there are no exceptions, boy." Philemon smiled gently. "Don't look so wary! You may find it odd the first few times, but soon you will be as much at home with us as everyone else is."

CHAPTER TWO

Philemon led Onesimus through the door and the pleasant odor of olives met the newcomer's nose as he was led toward the center of the room. Scattered throughout the room were stone pillar-like olive presses.

"The harvesters bring the olives into the pressing house where they are washed and ground into a thick paste in the millwheels," Philemon explained. "Then the paste is spread on those racks over there and the racks are put in the presses where, in a process you needn't worry about, the oil is forced out of the paste and collected for export.

"There are many wagonloads of olives that come in during the harvest and it's a good thing that the longer you wait to do the pressing the more oil you get! Those wagons need a place to wait their turn and that's why the walls are moveable," he explained as he placed a hand on a seemingly solid wall and pushed. The wall swung upward as Philemon walked outward, walking his hands down the wall until beams dropped from the wall to the ground, holding the wall up and out of the way, and creating a shady spot with a roof where a wagon-load of olives would be poised and readied to be emptied.

It wasn't until light flooded through the wall/roof that Onesimus realized there had been plenty of light to see inside the windowless room.

Startled, he blurted, "Where did the light come from before the wall was moved?"

Philemon chuckled, "Look up, boy! THAT is something I devised myself!"

Tilting his head back, Onesimus gasped as he looked up at the roof. There before his bewildered eyes was a hole cut into the roof above him. Around the hole were wooden beams about six-feet tall and resting on those beams was a second roof. That roof was larger than the hole below it, creating an overhang of several feet. Light was streaming through the gap, creating natural lighting for the building while preventing rain from entering; except during the rare, torrential wind-driven *horizontal rain*.

"Now then," Philemon continued. "It's time to see where you will be working and just what you will be doing."

He led Onesimus to a table and stool located near the presses, across the room from the noisy millwheels. "You will sit here and keep track of the wagonloads of harvested olives brought in, the number of amphorae of oil shipped, and the costs and profits accrued. I have a system of accounting that, like the lifted roof, is of my own design. It shouldn't take you long to learn it . . . the method is simple enough and you don't seem simple at all, so it should be easy for you," he laughed.

Onesimus soon found that Philemon was right. His accounting system was indeed *simple* and easy to learn and to use. It consisted mostly of one large scroll and two reed styli, one dipped in a well of black ink made from lamp soot and one dipped in a well of red-hued ink made from iron oxide. The red reed was used to record expenditures, such as cartage and shipping costs, and household, and maintenance expenses. The black reed recorded income from the sale of oil.

"Most merchants use wax tablets that can be smoothed over and metal styli, but I wish to keep my records for a long time. So, I use ink and scrolls instead," Philemon explained.

At a glance a knowledgeable clerk could find any expense or profit just by looking for either black or red ink.

After listening to the master explain his system and quite a lengthy time practicing making entries in the scroll, Onesimus was cheered to hear the master say, "Well enough for right now, Useful one! It's time for the midday meal and I am certainly ready! I think if we don't go in soon, I shall find myself eyeing your arm and wondering if it's meaty enough!"

With a laugh, Philemon led the way out of the pressing house toward his residence. As they approached, he waved toward the back of the house and said, "Just follow the others. You'll find food and fellowship in the cookhouse. Report back to the presshouse after the meal and I'll show you what I want you to do for the rest of the day."

Onesimus saw several people moving toward a small structure behind the main house. They were chatting and laughing and he thought to himself they certainly didn't seem much like the unhappy and sometimes surly slaves his family owned. These slaves acted more like freemen and friends. He shook his head as he joined them as they entered the warm room fragrant with the smell of fresh-baked bread.

As Onesimus stepped inside, Justin moved to his side and spoke loudly, "Everyone, please greet our newest arrival, Onesimus! He will be working in the pressing house counting olives and denarii."

Everyone glanced his way and murmured short greetings while continuing to work their way toward the long central table where food was laid out as you would expect to find around a family table. Onesimus was awed at the great variety of foods being offered. Besides the fresh bread he could smell, there was olive oil and salt to dip it in, two large pots of stew, ewers of goat's milk, bowls of olives and bowls of fresh vegetables from the garden.

Noticing his stunned look, a female slave spoke up. "It's much better here than it was at my original owners' home! There we ate bread and thin soup three times a day and were glad to get it. Here, fresh vegetables and milk are always plentiful. And sometimes there's even fruit to sweeten the meal. I am deeply grateful to God for the master! He saved my life when he bought me."

After a short pause she seemed to realize she had forgotten something. "Oh!" she said. "I'm sorry. My name is Apollonia. I'm one of the cooks. I've been a slave for eight years and have been here for three of them. I don't believe the master ever sells off any slaves." She touched her veiled head as her clear gray eyes gazed steadily into his.

Struck with her unusual eyes and comely figure, Onesimus struggled to find a relevant response. He finally settled on, "Well, it certainly smells like you know what you're doing!"

He was rewarded with a shy smile and a wooden plate.

He saw that the slaves who had filled their plates were waiting quietly and had not yet begun eating, so he too sat and waited. After the last of the slaves' plates been filled and the last slave had been seated, Justin rose to his feet and gave a short prayer of thanksgiving to the God of Israel for the bountiful food and the kind master they all worked for. He finished by asking God to bless the master and his business as well as the food. After a hearty 'Amen' they all began to eat.

Onesimus was beginning to realize that every mundane activity performed in this household might very well have some sort of prayer attached to it and he began to wonder how many of his fellow slaves were "true believers" and how many were just going along to keep the peace.

The questions flew at him from all sides and he tried to answer all of them as best he could. Was he native to the area or a captured foreigner? How had he, obviously educated and polished, wound up a slave? When they heard that his father had wasted the family fortune and then sold his son into slavery to pay his debts, around the table male heads shook while the women sighed, as they were all too familiar with the state of being of secondary importance, and love betrayed.

It seemed only a short time before Justin stood and declared, "Midday is done. Please return to your duties." Everyone stood and started for the door. Each knew where they belonged and their assigned tasks. Even Onesimus knew where his *usefulness* lay this day.

The rest of the day passed as he knew it would. He entered explanations, numbers in red and black, and he counted and he read over bills of lading and receipts. It wouldn't have taken quite so long, but thoughts of Apollonia's clear gray eyes and gentle smile kept intruding on everything he did.

He worked until his eyes felt like sandstone and his back ached with fatigue. Just as he was working up his courage to ask the master if he could take a short break, Philemon called out, "Enough! The sun is almost down and I am beginning to covet your arm again. Let us leave off for tonight and I will see you tomorrow at the Lord's Day meeting."

With that, he clapped Onesimus on the back and walked out the door, leaving Onesimus to decide how much storing of equipment to do and how much could be safely left out on his table.

CHAPTER THREE

The evening meal, served in the slaves' quarters, was simple but delicious with cheeses from the midday meal and bread as well as a large bowl of figs, grapes, parsnips, and other fruits and vegetables. Onesimus was pleasantly surprised at the quality of the wine available. Remembering the meals and posca (or vinegar mixed with water) his family had provided for their slaves, he realized again that he had been sold into a home that put his family's *adequate* treatment of slaves to shame.

Beyond the good food and wine, there was a level of camaraderie among the slaves that fostered a sense of family within Onesimus.

"Useful One," Justin called out during the meal. "Tell us more about yourself. We know what brought you to this sorry state..." A tittering among the women and low chuckling among the men let Onesimus know that the phrase "this sorry state" was not exactly how his fellow-slaves felt about this household. "So tell us of your boyhood pranks and the exploits you committed and suffered so we may see more of the real Onesimus."

Onesimus shifted on the bench and leaned into the table as he considered which adventure he should share this night.

His was a typical boyhood, ripe with many tales of perilous undertakings that would amuse and entertain the friendly listener. His only problem was choosing the right one. After a few moments for consideration, he began.

"When I was about five or six, our home mysteriously began to be home to a large family of mice. My father went out and found a couple of healthy-but-hungry-looking cats to come live with us and cut down the unruly population. They did their part well and began at once to chase down and devour many of the rodents. They were very impressive in their hunting prowess and were amazing in their obvious relish of those miserable little creatures. In fact, the cats enjoyed the mice so much we never had to feed them and they quickly grew plump."

He paused here, ordering his thoughts and preparing for the next revelation.

"In fact, they liked them so much that I began to wonder what was so special about the mice." As he paused to take a breath the men started to grin and most of the women paled. "I laid my plans carefully and began to watch the cats intently, just waiting my chance. My diligence paid off when I was able to watch one of the cats capture and begin to torture one of those unfortunate vermin. As soon as the poor creature was exhausted enough to handle, I rushed to pick it up. To the dismay of the successful hunter, I popped it in my mouth and bit down. Although I immediately gave it back to the cat she evinced no desire to complete her meal. To this day I don't understand what is so special about a mouthful of mouse!"

The chorus of guffaws and dismayed sounds around the table was gratifying to the storyteller and he sat back with a small grin lurking at the corners of his mouth.

"Well," Justin sputtered as he struggled to contain his laughter, "I guess that will teach me to ask for a story from a newcomer without warning!"

Apollonia closed her eyes and shook her head but Onesimus noticed her shoulders were shaking slightly and her lips were turned upward in a secret grin. For Onesimus, that was reward enough.

After the clearing away was finished and the basins and ewers of water were placed on the tables for the morning, the women left for their own quarters and groups of friends began to talk together or play games. A young man Onesimus took to be Vitus (the aroma gave him away!) invited him to join his group that was playing Tali and Tropa. He remembered playing the game with Protos, so it wasn't long before Onesimus had re-learned the rules of the game and was able to throw the sticks and total his score almost as fast as the experienced players.

Slowly, the smoking olive-oil lamps throughout the room were extinguished and as darkness descended Justin approached him and spoke quietly. "Tomorrow is Lord's Day. We do no work. Instead we spend the day in worshiping the God of Israel and His Son, Yeshua. All must attend the meeting tomorrow morning—whether you believe or not—but in the afternoon non-believers are welcome to participate in the spiritual discussions that follow the morning assembly or to participate in quiet pastimes."

Onesimus made his way to his couch and, with a rustle of the sweet-smelling straw filler, stretched out and covered himself with the slightly worn woolen coverlet that provided plenty of warmth and comfort as he drifted off to sleep.

He was in a ship with his father and brother. They were having a fine time together, but a storm was coming. The sky darkened and the waves rose high, towering over their vessel. It wasn't long before the boat was tossing as if it were a small stick on the Tiber. The sailors were cursing and calling on the gods for help. There was a loud screech and CRACK!; the stern of the ship was torn away and sunk quickly taking half the crew to their doom. He knew there was no hope. There were only a few seconds in which to grab something that would float before the bow of the ship followed the stern to its watery grave. He grabbed the nearest thing, a small beam that had been ripped from the hull and flung through the air onto the deck.

Suddenly he tasted salt water and his brother and father were clinging to the board with him. But the weight of three grown men was too much for the little beam. Soon Protos and his father were crying that they would all drown if something weren't done quickly. He heard his father shouting to Protos, "Push him off! Better that you and I should live and Onesimus perish than that we all die!"

Onesimus was struggling with his brother and was about to lose his grip on the board when he suddenly heard the ship's bell ringing... but that couldn't be... the bell was at the bottom of the Great Sea now... then where was that...?

He jerked awake and realized the ship's bell was actually the rising bell.

Justin was walking through the quarters ringing a bell and shouting, "Rise up! Rise up! Give glory to the God of the Universe and praise to His Son. The day has dawned and we may yet serve Him another day!"

It was a few seconds before Onesimus was awake enough to open his eyes and realize where he was. When he did he saw first, Justin—walking between the tables and the beds, reciting something that sounded foreign, as Onesimus imagined Hebrew holy words might sound. Then he saw the tables laden with basins and ewers where every man, upon arising, washed himself before donning his clothes.

When everyone was attired and the basins emptied and put away, the door was opened to the women who came in and gathered with the men as Justin led them all in a prayer of thanksgiving.

Some light clean-up followed amid quiet discussions concerning their work, the master and his family, the coming meeting, and life in general.

Dismayed, Onesimus realized that the women had brought no food and he wondered about breaking fast and hoped an all-day holy-day fast wasn't part of this new religion.

Nevertheless, he set to with a will and was wiping up spilled water on the tables and listening to the different conversations swirling around him when he realized there was one fellow who had been watching him with subtle intensity.

He was older than Onesimus and slightly stooped. His head was nearly bald but his scalp wasn't bare. It was covered with freckles and when Onesimus' eyes met his eyes, the man smiled and spoke.

"Your labor commends you. Are you a follower of the Christ?"

"No, sir," Onesimus replied. "I have never known anyone who was and I have never had the chance to learn about this new religion."

"It really isn't new … it's only a new branch of the religion of the Jews," came the response. "You will have many opportunities to learn more as long as you live here."

From across the room came the announcement, "It's time to go. People are coming up the road."

Onesimus watched as the room began to empty and the older man he'd been talking to spoke once again. "I'm Alpheus. I am Justin's brother and work as a wheelwright for the Master. When the wheels are rolling right, I help Justin or anyone else who needs me." He took Onesimus by the arm and led him toward the door.

"But come, now. It's time for your first lesson about the Chosen One."

CHAPTER FOUR

O nesimus followed the others away from the back of the house and into the front yard. As he looked around he saw that the tables from the kitchen where they had eaten yesterday had been moved outside.

As he looked up and down the road he could see five or six family groups carrying baskets and greeting one another on the way. When they arrived they put their baskets on the tables. Happy greetings floated on the air as the women greeted one another with gladsome tones and cheek kisses; the men did the same.

The air was full of chatter and laughter, but nothing could hide the joyful shout that erupted from Philemon's mouth as he spied another man walking alone toward the gathering. The man was small, perhaps only one-and-a-half meters tall, and bent in the back as if he carried a heavy load on his shoulders. His hair was plentiful, sticking out all around a balding center like rust-colored wires from a curry-comb. His eyes were steady and greenish-gray and his arms were muscular.

"Priscus! How wonderful to see you! We weren't expecting you today, but I'm glad you're here."

The man he greeted looked up and grinned as he entered the yard. "Philemon! How good to see you again!" he said with enthusiasm. "I spent all day yesterday visiting the body of Christ at the home of Marcus-the-fuller and wanted to spend a little time with you before I travel on. Even though they entreated me to stay with them through Lord's Day I really wanted to see you all, so I left late yesterday afternoon and walked into the night, bedding down by the roadside so I could reach your church this morning."

"Well, you not only arrived in time for the meeting, my friend. You got here in time to break your fast with us too!" Philemon answered.

Everyone, slave and free, men and women, were taking food from the baskets and sitting down on the ground or on the porch but no one was yet eating.

Onesimus too, selected a choice piece of chicken and a handful of grapes and sat down beside Justin under a nearby tree.

A pause in the conversations signaled a change in atmosphere as Philemon raised his hands in the air and began to give thanks to the God of Israel for the food and for this gathering of saints. He asked for blessings on the food and on those who brought the food and he asked that God would shower knowledge of Himself upon those who had not yet believed.

After he had uttered "Amen!" everyone began to eat and laugh and fellowship together. The man with the bristly red hair came up to Onesimus and spoke. "I understand you are new to this household," he said genially. "Are you finding comfort here? Are you being treated well?"

Having observed how close Priscus and Philemon were, Onesimus would never have answered differently than he did even if he *were* being treated badly. "It is a fine household! The Master is fair and the food is good. Much better than the food we supplied for our slaves!"

Priscus' eyebrows shot upward but he was too polite to inquire.

Onesimus cocked his head to one side and a small, wry smile played around his lips. "My father had to raise the payment for a bad debt in a hurry and I was his solution."

Priscus nodded solemnly and patted his arm.

In a little while all were finished breaking fast and began to enter the house. Because of the size of the crowd, the slaves present (many of whom came with their masters and mistresses) sat on the porch outside open windows and listened closely. Onesimus had a curious nature and really wanted to miss nothing of this strange cult, so he sat as closely as he could to a window that looked directly into the main gathering room. It didn't hurt matters that Apollonia sat nearby.

At first, a deep silence prevailed both within the room and on the porch. Then, slowly, the people began to sing. Onesimus listened closely as first one and then another voice joined in praises to God. A girl of about fourteen started the song with a high, sweet melody and words that sounded like the Scriptures Justin was so fond of quoting.

"My soul magnifies the Lord. May the God of Israel be exalted in all I do. Glory and honor adorns his head and righteousness bedecks his throne."

A bass voice and an alto added their harmonies to the song and soon many others were joining in. While only the first young woman sang words, the others hummed or intoned harmonies that fit closely and without seam to everything she sang. A chill rose on Onesimus' arms as he realized these people seemed to be singing a spontaneous song in perfect harmony.

As the song faded out, almost everyone within the room and on the porch began praying quietly—but aloud—and soon a young man of twenty or twenty-one began to speak louder than the others who immediately quieted so that he could be heard.

"Thus saith the Lord God of Israel. 'I have seen your works and know you. You worship me in joy, but I say to you there are soon coming times when only those who can worship me in sorrow will stand. Stand, therefore, and determine to worship me in sorrow as well as in joy.' Thus saith the Lord God of Israel."

Silence reigned for several minutes as people absorbed what had been said. As if to confirm what had been spoken, an elderly woman slowly rose to her feet.

"Please pray for Antipas. He was in the marketplace last week when he was accosted by three men. These men seemed to know he was a follower of the Way and beat him unmercifully. He cannot rise from his bed and prays only for the pain to cease. Pray that God will deliver him from his pain and will either heal him or take him home quickly."

Everyone who had heard the woman's plea began to pray and the prayer quickly evolved into a time of praise again. After that, another song arose.

When the song was finished, Philemon asked, "Has anyone heard from Chronion and Ennathus?"

A concert of shaking heads indicated that no one had heard from the couple in question.

"The Lord is saying we need to pray for them," Philemon continued.

A very tall, skinny man rose to his feet. His black hair was trimmed short in the Roman style and he wore a white toga edged with green. He lifted his hands and began to pray. "Father, in obedience to you we pray for our brother and sister. We do not know where they are or what has happened, but we know you never require baseless prayers from your people. Protect them wherever they are and bring them home to us safe. In the name of your Holy Son, Yeshua, Amen."

The meeting continued with people speaking, and singing and praying in turn. The young woman who began the first song spoke up, "I need somewhere to stay. My father found out I was coming here and told me I was endangering my family by turning my back on his gods. He said that was why he'd been having so much bad luck in the marketplace and he demanded that I either repudiate the Messiah or leave his house."

An older woman stood up beside her and put her arms around her. "Come stay with us, Zoe. You can use the room my daughter had until she married and we can use the company." The woman brushed the tears from Zoe's cheeks and the girl smiled in return.

Suddenly a man and woman of about thirty came running onto the porch and into the house. The man was carrying a small child who lay limply across his arms.

"Quickly! Pray for Felix, please! We were leaving our home to come here and a Centurion came by on his horse. He was galloping along and Felix ran in front of him. The horse knocked him down and stepped right on him. He's been like this ever since!"

A group of believers gathered around the couple and several reached out and put their hands on the child. Even a few of the slaves moved inward to take part. From where Onesimus sat, nothing of the couple or the child could be seen as they stood within that circle of caring, praying individuals. It was only a matter of seconds when a murmur arose and the circle parted so that Onesimus had a clear view of the boy and his parents. But now, the boy was sitting up in his father's arms and squirming to get down.

"Want down!" he shouted imperiously. "Want down NOW!"

Praise again broke forth and Onesimus was at a loss to understand what had just happened. The child was obviously in a serious condition when the group began to pray and he was obviously NOT in a serious condition when they finished. But Onesimus had no idea what brought about the change.

As the rejoicing continued, another slave about Onesimus' age tapped him on the arm and whispered, "That's Chronion and Ennathus!"

A few minutes later, Priscus stood and smiled at those around him. "I bring a message of warning and encouragement from the Most High God.

"Brothers I am most concerned about the coming days. While persecution and trials have so far been scattered, I see that it won't be long before we too will be hunted and hounded. Rumors already abound that we are cannibals, child eaters, and no better than vermin.

"Beyond the slanders from the outside, there are some difficulties from within our ranks as well. Paulus has written several letters to counter these problems and I would like to tell you what he says about those among us who say the Christ has already returned. He tells us first that they are wrong. Christ will not come back until after that evil person, the Son of Perdition, is revealed. That man will set himself up as a deliverer and will deceive many. He will speak blasphemies and will seek to change times and seasons. Many will look to him for deliverance from the evil days of that time.

"He will make peace and cause all men to dwell in comfort and safety. And when they are completely off their guard, he will break the peace and will commit war against God and against the people of God.

"Many people will be deceived by him. So deceived in fact, that they will obey when he creates a blasphemous image in the very Temple of Jerusalem and demand worship from the people. He will proclaim himself to be God!"

A shifting and shuffling ensued with murmured comments from the listeners.

"Our affections must not waver, our hearts must stand firm. Only the Christ, the Chosen One, He who died for our sins and rose again on the third day... only He is to be worshiped!

"Perilous times are upon us. The prophecy through Petros was truly from God Himself. We must learn quickly that we cannot understand every event that takes place in our lives. We cannot doubt the love of God because of evil things that may happen to us in this temporary jar of clay we now inhabit.

"We must stand firm against all the wiles of our great enemy... the enemy of Christ... and refuse to be lead away from the Scriptures of Truth. Whatever we see in our flesh is not necessarily of God. Satan can deceive anyone who takes their eyes from the Holy One and our only safety lies in awaiting the return of our own Christ even when another Christ arises who demands our worship!

"Understand that when this evil one raises himself up, it is *then* that we must begin to watch for the coming of *our* Christ. Christ will NOT appear before all that has been written in the Scriptures has been fulfilled.

'And while we await the coming of the Lord and live among the wolves who would seek our destruction, we must comfort one another with the words of promise.'"

The meeting continued until the sun was high overhead. There were more healings, more words from different people, even a slave boy of about twelve stood up and told about a dream he had had.

"I was asleep last night shortly before cock crow, when the Lord sent me a dream," he began. "I dreamed that two young men and an older man had been on a ship that broke apart in a heavy storm. They found a board and all three were clinging to this board when the older man told one of the younger men to force the other man off the board because their combined weight was sinking the board. The Lord spoke to me then and said, 'Tell the dream at the gathering for someone there needs to hear it. He is in great pain and must know that I, the Lord, know everything that has happened to him. I know and I care and I am working all these things out for his good and my Glory.' That's when I awoke."

Onesimus had listened in amazement as this young stranger recounted exactly portions of the nightmare he had had just before waking. As the boy took his seat again, Onesimus touched his hand to his face and found his cheeks were wet. He quickly wiped away the tears and hoped no one had noticed.

When the assembly ended, the crowd of people began to move into the front yard and toward the remaining baskets of food which were still on the tables. Onesimus stood in amazement as he saw the master walk directly up to Alpheus and offer him one of the chicken legs he was carrying in his hands.

Alpheus accepted the offering and laughed at something Philemon said to him.

Turning to Onesimus, Philemon then said, "Come, Useful One! Come help yourself to some of Felicitatis's wonderful chicken and the bread of a most excellent baker named Erastus!"

It seemed there would be no class distinctions during the second meal and discussion any more than there had been during the gathering.

Even after the earlier meal breaking the fast, there still was plenty for everyone. Along with the chicken (which did prove to be excellent) and the crusty, fragrant bread there were baskets of grapes, olives, figs, raisins and dates. There were also baked eggs and cold lamb and fish that had been wrapped in grape leaves and roasted. All in all, a feast of magnificent proportions had been brought together for the enjoyment of all those who came to the meeting.

Talk centered around the words of Brother Priscus and those who had sung and prophesied.

Onesimus had carefully observed the actions of his fellow slaves and realized that eating heartily and listening to the discussions was not only allowed but expected. For a little while, he listened in on a group that was talking about the dream of the young slave but he found it too disturbing so he wandered off and stood listening to a group of five or six men who were talking about the meaning or identity of the Son of Perdition Priscus had spoken of. While they were careful not to name him it was obvious from the discussion that many believed the Roman Caesar to be that man.

Onesimus was startled by a touch on his arm as a skinny man of dark and wrinkled skin was expounding on the possible identity of that man, "Well, I know of no other person this man of lawlessness could possibly be than . . ."

"My friend! I'm afraid we were so hungry we began breaking our fast before we could even exchange names!"

Jumping slightly, Onesimus turned to see Brother Priscus standing beside him. "However, I understand from our host that you are the Useful One . . . Onesimus. Is that correct? You know my name, I am Priscus. We didn't get a chance to visit much before the service. Are you a part of the Way?"

"Yes sir," Onesimus replied. "That is, I do know your name. But as to the Way, I know not of what you are speaking."

"Ah! Well. If you were of the Way, you would know. Therefore, it is obvious you haven't yet found your way to the Way!" Priscus laughed at his own little joke. "So what did you think of our gathering today?"

Brother Priscus led Onesimus over to the porch and slid down against the house wall, patting the porch floor beside him. "Come. Sit and let us talk."

"I've several questions, if you don't mind," Onesimus began.

"Ask away. We can never gain knowledge if we never ask a question."

"First, you say you came from visiting the body of . . . Christ? Why do you visit a dead man?"

Priscus chuckled. "No. The Body of Christ isn't His physical body. He was resurrected in His body and now He lives in Heaven with His Father, Yahweh God. The Body of Christ is the group of believers in any certain place. For instance, THESE believers are all part of the Body of Christ. They are called the Body of Christ at Colossae. And not all members of the Body of Christ at Colossae meet here in Philemon's house. There are several meetings just like this going on around the city."

Onesimus nodded. Not comprehending completely what Brother Priscus was saying but grasping enough to continue with his questioning.

"Fine. The main question I have concerns my own curiosity. Why would any group of people choose to follow an invisible God when those in power may be working toward a time when they would kill anyone who dared ally themselves with him? It seems a foolhardy thing to do. Just look at that man you prayed for today who was beaten by a group of thugs. How long will you continue to follow this God if persecution becomes your daily lot?"

"It's foolhardy only if this is the only life we will have," Priscus replied. "If we have no hope beyond the grave, then we are the most miserable of all creatures, because you are right. Those in power would take our lives, our property and our dignity without hesitation. But we have a hope. Yeshua promised His followers that He was going back to Heaven to prepare a place for all of us to come to. He told us that we who follow Him will live forever with Him and His Father in Heaven. His resurrection from the dead to new life is His proof that He was telling the truth. Many people saw Him die and many of those same people saw Him alive again three days later. Paulus himself was called to Him by Yeshua's own voice after spending time railing against The Way and I was persuaded through the words of Paulus.

"Our bodies are just..." Priscus hesitated as he looked around them. He bent over and picked up a small clod of dried clay that had dropped from someone's sandal. "Our bodies are just..." he pinched the clay between his thumb and forefinger and it crumbled away into dust. "Dust. WE are not our bodies... our bodies are simply clay prisons that hold us until we are set free of them to dwell with our Master forever."

Onesimus nodded. "I see what you are saying. I have been thinking about your question... am I a part of the Way. I know now of what you are speaking, but I am not ready to follow your ... Master. Even so, I do promise to think about it."

Brother Priscus nodded soberly and patted Onesimus once more. "Yes. It is always wise to consider what you have learned and to make an informed decision. But be certain you do not wait too long to conclude your deliberations ... it is dangerous to delay."

A tall, willowy woman called to Priscus. "Brother Priscus! It was so good to hear you today! I hope you will stay in the region for a while."

Priscus smiled and replied, "I'm afraid the Spirit has called me away to another region, but I shall return as soon as He allows it, Sister Marcella." He then arose as effortlessly as he had sat down and bade Onesimus a polite goodbye as he made his farewells and headed toward the road.

CHAPTER FIVE

Onesimus and Protos were playing Tali and Tropa and Onesimus was ahead when a huge mouse dashed across the sticks that he had just tossed. The sticks were all stirred and the points that had been lying there were gone before they could be tallied. Protos, who had only been behind by a few points, grabbed the mouse and swallowed him whole. Then he grabbed the sticks and began to chant, "I win! I win! You lose! You lose!" Onesimus balled up his fist in preparation to beat the tar out of his older brother.

"Blessed be the Lord God of Israel. Praise Him, sun and moon; praise Him all you shining stars!"

The strange words, uttered by a stranger's voice woke him more certainly than the ringing bell ever could. Onesimus rolled from his couch and heeled his eyes with his hands until he saw spots of light.

Remembering his dream, he shook his head and wondered why the mouse-eating caper had entered his dreams tonight instead of last night. He shrugged to himself. Ah, well . . . you could never tell about how the gods would play in your mind.

Others were already standing at the wash basins and splashing water in their faces. Some were tending to their whiskers and others were pulling on fresh clothing. Some had already seated themselves on their couches and were awaiting a chance to begin eating the flat loaves of rye bread and cheese that had been prepared in the main kitchen and delivered earlier.

He prepared for the day and joined the others around the table.

Justin spoke to him with a smile. "The master will want to get you started today, so as soon as you have eaten I would suggest you report to the olive press." He looked down at Onesimus' feet and saw that the Useful One was barefoot.

"Oh! That will never do! The master takes great pride in supplying his house servants with ample clothing, including two pairs of sandals every year. He expects them to go shod at all times they are about his business."

"Of course. I simply prefer to go barefooted while I am here . . . I would never think of appearing before the master unshod," Onesimus replied.

Another slave, known as Barsabas was listening and interjected, "Hmmmph! Well, it will save the leather!" They laughed together and prepared to begin their varied duties.

The day passed quickly and it wasn't long before Onesimus really did see how simple the two-colored inks and scroll his master had shown him were to follow and use and how permanent those records were. By the mid-day break, Onesimus was beginning to get a pretty good picture of his master's extensive business. He had learned that the sale of olive oil from his master's groves produced enough income over and above its shipping costs to support a household that included not only his wife, Apphia, and two children but a mother-in-law who was widowed and the master's father who had left reason behind and lived a protected life in a small house near the olive grove with an attendant. Onesimus was just reaching the latest year's records when Philemon appeared.

"Come, Useful One! It's time to partake of some excellent food and drink before continuing with this plodding work!" He called with good humor.

Clapping a friendly hand on Onesimus' shoulder, Philemon guided him toward the kitchen of the main house, adding, "I understand today's feast is barley loaves fresh baked and apples from Ignatius' own orchard, (he nodded at the orchard across the road), and fresh vegetables grown in the kitchen garden."

The very thought of all that wonderful food set the slave's mouth to watering and when he stepped into the building and smelled the powerful and succulent odor of the hot barley bread drifting through the air he thought he would faint with hunger. Lost in his tasks, he had had no idea how long he had toiled and how ready his poor stomach was for a refill until that moment. Onesimus hurried to the table and sat down. Thoughtlessly, he began to reach for a steaming platter of barley loaves but a hand streaked out from the person next to him and covered his. At first, Onesimus was startled and then a little piqued. Then he realized that, while everyone was seated, no one was eating. He remembered other meals and glanced at the owner of the hand. It was Alpheus and as Onesimus looked on, Alpheus closed his eyes and began to speak.

"God and Father of all believers, we thank You for Your great provision for us and we ask that you will bless this food for our nourishment. Help us always to remember from whence this bounty comes and to be grateful. Amen."

A sudden flurry of hands reaching for serving platters informed the newcomer that it was now time to enjoy the wonderful repast set before him.

The food was, as promised, delicious and plentiful and Onesimus realized that he would never go hungry as long as he worked in this household . . . and for this he gave his first quiet thanks to the God Who had brought him to this place.

All too soon it was time to return to the scrolls and accounts he had left, but he set to willingly, knowing his lot could be much worse than it was. It was especially clear when he paused before entering the olive press to gaze out through the olive orchards that surrounded the house on three sides. There he saw the field hands laboring vigorously under the hot, midday sun. Even they had it better than many slaves, though. They all worked for a master that cared for them. This was demonstrated by the fact that each group of slaves had a jar of fresh water with them from which they could drink at any time.

When he considered what he as a slave might have been required to do . . . when he remembered what his father's slaves were required to do . . . he felt grateful to Philemon. And yet, not just to Philemon. *Just thank the Fates . . .* his thoughts began. Then he stopped. He knew better. He knew there was Someone besides those minor gods that he should acknowledge as the Master of his fate. The slave boy's account of his dream had convinced him of that ... but he wasn't yet ready to take that step. After all, if that Someone was the same Someone Priscus had spoken of the day before, and if times as difficult as he described were truly coming, taking that step could cost Onesimus his very life ... and, he argued with himself, he just wasn't ready to risk everything for Someone he wasn't even sure existed.

He shook himself free of his contemplative mood and stepped into the olive-fragrant room, moving quickly to his desk and the task of comprehending every small detail of his master's vast business accounts.

Mentally shifting into accounting mode, he opened the scroll he had been working on when he was called to lunch. He had been working steadily long enough to lose track of the time when, with a shout and a noisy crashing, a boy about twelve years old came bounding through the doorway, his black curls bouncing wildly on his head as if they were trying to escape the mayhem brewing beneath their bed and his tanned arms glistening with sweat and covered with a fine greenish dusting of weed seed.

The boy began vigorously brushing his arms as he spoke, "Have you seen my father? I've been playing hide and seek with Blandina and now I need to show Father what I've found!"

Onesimus began to smile. The boy reminded him of himself at that age. He must be Quintin, Philemon's son.

"I'm sorry," he replied. "I'm not sure where he is. He spent the morning here with me but he said something about checking the groves this afternoon. He probably isn't too far into them. If you hurry, you might be able to catch up to him."

"Did you find him yet?" a young girl shouted as she skipped into the room. The single long, blond braid that hung down her back and the huge sea-green eyes that sat surrounded by thick, brown lashes in the middle of her freckled eleven-year-old face contrasted mightily with the boy's black curls, sun-darkened skin and brown eyes. Still, their familial resemblance screamed out to him from their almost-straight noses, full lips, flat cheekbones, pointed chins and their similar, slightly chubby physiques.

This has got to be Blandina. Onesimus thought as he heard Quintin's reply.

"He thinks Father is in the groves. Let's go see if we can find him."

As they pelted off through the sun-washed meadow, laughing and chattering more like best friends than siblings, Onesimus sighed and turned back to his scrolls. He remembered that kind of camaraderie with his own brother . . . until the money problems started mounting up.

As he sat upon his stool and thought about his recent past, he could place exactly when he knew he was no longer considered equal to the "Preeminent One."

It seemed as if it had been months, but in reality it had only been about two weeks since the day he came in for the evening meal and no one would look him in the eyes. His mother, strangely enough, was absent from the table completely, his father spoke to Protos almost incessantly . . . as if he were afraid that if he was silent, the sacrificial lamb would grow a tongue and begin to speak.

He never spoke his second son's name that night. At the end of the meal, his father glanced at him and quickly away before saying, "I need to see you privately when you are done." His father then rose from the table and left the room.

"What is going on?" Onesimus asked his brother, but his brother simply stared at his plate unhappily. After a few seconds Protos rose and, murmuring excuses quickly left the room.

There was still a goodly amount of food left on Onesimus' plate, but suddenly he wasn't hungry. It seemed as if his stomach had been filled by a huge rock and his mouth seemed filled with sand, making it impossible for him to swallow. He left the table and went to find his father walking the grounds of their home, his hands fisted at his sides and a frown that threatened to break his face into two pieces because of the depths of the crease it had created.

Quickly, Onesimus cast about in his memory for anything he might have done that would bring that look to his father's face. He could remember seeing that frown twice before. Once, when he was about ten and got into a terrible fight with a neighbor's son who, quoting his father, had called Onesimus' father a "spendthrift fool". He had never told his father the cause of the fight. The other time he had seen it was when in the throes of youthful passion, he had burst into his father's presence and declared with all the abandon of a thirteen-year-old that he loved Afra, one of his mother's slaves, and had every intention of marrying her immediately, with or without parental blessing.

It went without saying that no good thing had ever come to Onesimus when his father wore that face!

"You have been a good son to me," his father began. It sounded like a speech he had rehearsed until he no longer had to think of the words as he said them. "I wish there were an easier way to say this but there isn't. So ... I guess I will say it simply and directly. I've been a fool and a wastrel. I've squandered all my wealth on false friends and dangerous pastimes and now it comes back to me to wreak a terrible vengeance. There are men who need to be paid and I've nothing left to pay them with. I have sold everything I own that I can possibly sell ... even this home ... and there is only one way I can raise the rest of the money I need to satisfy these beasts. I must sell one of my two most prized possessions. I want you to get your affairs in order because within a week, you are to be sold to satisfy this terrible debt.

"Always remember I love you, son. But there is nothing I can do."

And with that, his father turned his back and walked away. And Onesimus clenched his fists in rage and started after him, "Father! Father! Are you selling Protos as well? Do we mean so little to you?"

His father stopped and stared at the ground at his feet. He simply shook his head, "I must have an heir. Protos is the rightful heir. He stays ... but you must go."

Recalling—no, *reliving*—that moment tore open a wound that had barely started to heal. He tried to will himself back to the present in a desperate effort to quench the maelstrom of feelings that threatened to overwhelm him in a horrific mix of pain, confusion, loss and rage. But coming back to the bitter reality of the present offered no shelter from his emotions. When he opened his eyes he was still seated in a stranger's olive press, studying a stranger's accounts and recording a stranger's business dealings.

Unable to deal with the fusillade of passions now raging within, Onesimus stood from the stool he was perched on and began to pace the room. Onesimus strode with fisted hands, moving from one end of the room to the opposite end and then reversing the process. It was true he was in deep pain from his treatment at his father's hands. But there was more ... so much more to his feelings. A vile and hateful jealousy toward his once-beloved brother had grown up in the last two weeks. As the pain had faded to a dull ache, the hatred and anger he felt toward both his brother and his father grew and consumed him every time he recalled the events of that foul night. Although Onesimus didn't comprehend it, a tree of bitterness was taking root in his heart and, if not removed soon, would become the center of his life.

When he found no relief from the stress, he moved out into the meadow behind the press and took off at a trot. He ran with no destination in mind. He was simply trying to outrun his feelings or make himself so tired he could return to his work and behave like an individual who hadn't been touched by the moon's evil influence. The exercise began to work. His blood began to beat hard in his veins, his breathing became harsh and soon he experienced the relief that runners call, "second wind". He trotted back to the olive press and re-entered the building, panting and somewhat sweaty but ready to return to his duties.

"Well! Nice to see you've returned," Philemon called out from his own table. "Imagine my thoughts when I came in and found you were missing!"

"I'm so sorry sir," Onesimus replied, deeply mindful that his behavior could merit a whipping. "I simply had to stretch my legs. I will gladly put in some extra time this evening to make up for the lost time."

Philemon shook his head. "Not necessary this time, young man. I can certainly understand how a healthy young fellow might need to take a little exercise to feel ready to tackle a lifetime's business. If you like, you may take a short span to exercise after lunch every day, if that will keep you productive and happy."

Onesimus felt a welling inside that corresponded to the unexpected tears that sprang into his eyes. He blinked and looked away but not quickly enough. He knew Philemon had seen.

Onesimus replied, "No sir. Thank you but I think I need to stay busy and think of other things if you don't mind."

Philemon shrugged and smiled. "Fine. Fine. Take a few minutes to gather yourself and wash up. Then we will continue with the work."

Onesimus hurried across the yard to the cistern near the kitchen. He drew up some water and splashed his face and under his arms. He poured the rest of the cool and refreshing water over his head, then, shaking his head vigorously like a dog, he strode back across the yard to the olive press and perched himself back on his stool.

Philemon glanced up with a slight frown of concern and returned to his work as his new slave settled in for an afternoon of accounts receivable and accounts payable.

He was beginning to think he'd made the best purchase of his lifetime with the acquisition of the Useful One.

CHAPTER SIX

Another Sunday came and Onesimus was as intrigued as ever with the worship of this new god.

While the gathering was very similar to the first one he had attended, Priscus was not there so after breaking the fast, the chattering group gathered and sat down in respectful silence while Philemon brought out a scroll and reverently unrolled it as he explained its origins.

"This is a copy of a letter sent by our dear brother Paulus to the believers at Galatia. Priscus left it for us when he was here last week. Our freedom to gather and worship is not guaranteed in this world. As you know, Paulus has been under arrest at Caesarea for two years now and many others have already been imprisoned. Some have even been killed for the Gospel of our Lord Christ Jesus. But our freedom is not of the body but of the soul. Our freedom was bought by the death of Yeshua whom we worship. And as our freedom from sin and evil was bought by His death, our freedom from the fear of death and from death itself was bought by His resurrection.

"As Brother Paulus said in a letter to the Body of Christ at Corinth, 'Where, o death is thy sting and where, o grave is thy victory?'"

Philemon began to read, "'So I say, let the Holy Spirit guide your lives. Then you won't be doing what your sinful nature craves. The sinful nature wants to do evil, which is just the opposite of what the Spirit wants. And the Spirit gives us desires that are the opposite of what the sinful nature desires. These two forces are constantly fighting each other, so you are not free to carry out your good intentions. But when you are directed by the Spirit, you are not under obligation to the law of Moses.

When you follow the desires of your sinful nature, the results are very clear: sexual immorality, impurity, lustful pleasures, idolatry, sorcery, hostility, quarreling, jealousy, outbursts of anger, selfish ambition, dissension, division, envy, drunkenness, wild parties and other sins like these. Let me tell you again, as I have before, that anyone living that sort of life will not inherit the Kingdom of God.

'But the Holy Spirit produces this kind of fruit in our lives: love, joy, peace, patience, kindness, goodness, faithfulness, gentleness and self-control. There is no law against these things!

'Those who belong to Christ Jesus have nailed the passions and desires of their sinful nature to His cross and crucified them there. Since we are living by the Spirit, let us follow the Spirit's leading in every part of our lives. Let us not become conceited, or provoke one another, or be jealous of one another.'"

Onesimus listened closely. Free of evil passions! Could one really be free of evil passions? He had such hatred and jealousy toward his brother and father!

He had a right! They had treated him so badly! Why would he want to feel anything but hatred and jealousy toward those vile men?

Philemon rolled up the scroll and began to speak. "We who are in the Way many times have seen the results of those passions from which Christ has set us free. Recall those who have torn apart their homes over unfounded jealousies and those who have sought vengeance against their believing neighbors by causing problems for them.

"Even those of us who serve the God of Heaven must wrestle with these passions. It is not that we never *feel* anger or bitterness or jealousy. It is that, when we begin to feel those things, we have a refuge in Christ Jesus. We can call upon Him and He will help us to guard our hearts and minds from these things as the writer of Proverbs instructed us. His Spirit will guide us in worship and praise and guide us away from dwelling on these vile things. If there was no danger to the believer, Paulus would not have written these words urging us to live differently.

"The more often we call upon the Holy Spirit to help us overcome these feelings the stronger we become in resisting them and the weaker the wrong emotions' hold on us becomes.

"Take heed. Many have stated clearly that our enemy, the accuser of the brothers, wanders the earth looking for souls he may devour. It is in these evil times, when injustice and hatred of believers are becoming not only acceptable but encouraged that we must even more guard against becoming entrapped in the sinful emotions and acts Paulus lists here.

"Let us now pray that the Holy Spirit will continue to guard us and will move upon us to choose the Way over the common."

When the believers began to lift their hands and pray, Onesimus did something even he did not expect. He dipped his head and thought, "Yeshua. If you really are the God of Creation, reveal Yourself to me. If you can wipe out these vile hatreds, I might just give You my all."

After the midday meal, Onesimus and the other slaves spent the rest of the day quietly. Some sat around the table in the slaves' quarters and discussed Paulus' letter and Philemon's exhortations concerning it. A few cast lots together for personal items and several, including Onesimus, chose to take walks or other exercise and simply rest.

Onesimus walked out across the yard and into the edge of the olive groves. Directly in front of the Master's house, across the road lay Ignatius' apple orchard that had provided the apples he had enjoyed since he had arrived. It stretched away to his right. To his left across the road he saw fields of millet and wheat that waved in the summer breeze. His eyes beheld the beauty of the world while his mind insisted these things must be the work of a loving God and his soul cried out to know the truth concerning this Yahweh.

Finally he came to a small stream that seemed to create a natural border between Philemon's groves and a herd of sheep grazing in tall grass. He sat down with his back to an olive tree and closed his eyes. The clouds had dissipated and the warmth of the sun and the soft breeze began to soothe his tired heart and mind. The smell of wildflowers, grasses and olives mixed with the pungent presence of the sheep and created in his mind a haven where he could retreat from the realities of his life. He was so tired of these feelings . . . so tired of dreaming disturbing dreams of betrayal . . . so tired of mistrusting everyone . . . . Soon he became aware of sounds he never seemed to hear when his eyes were open. The wind made a soft hissing sound through the tall grass across the brook as the olive trees' branches brushed together, clicking and rattling. The ringing of the bell around the neck of the bellwether punctuated the bleats of a lamb and once in a while the voice of a ewe would float to him as she called for her baby and always, always the water of the trickling brook over stones created a music that edged him closer to a blessed rest. He was almost asleep when he heard wings and felt a sudden weight on his outstretched foot.

He started and opened one eye. Perched on his left foot was a dove. His snowy head was cocked to one side and he watched Onesimus with his beady left eye. Onesimus tilted his head slightly to the right and stared back at the bird. The dove shifted slightly, making Onesimus' foot dip and sway like a tree branch. Onesimus tipped his head to the left and continued to watch the bird.

After a short time the bird cooed just once and lifted off his perch. Instead of taking off in a soaring flight he flew in a straight line toward Onesimus' face yet the slave felt not the slightest worry about the claws and beak of the bird. He just sat there quiet as the bird flew close to his head, brushing his forehead with the tips of his wings in what seemed to be a blessing and then disappearing across the creek.

Chapter Seven

Onesimus lay quietly on his couch. It was late. He should be sleeping, getting ready for the workday ahead, but instead his head was filled with his strange visitation earlier that afternoon. His forehead still felt the brush of the dove's soft wing as if it had left a trail of some tangible substance as it passed by. A substance that was sweet and full of hope. What was the meaning of the visitation? Was it an answer to his prayer? As a good scholar he knew the significance of omens and portents.

If his feelings were reliable this omen was for good, not evil . . . but were his feelings reliable? He would have to wait and see.

The harvest was beginning in the morning and he knew he had to be alert to keep up with the arriving carts full of olives. Using a system he had barely had time to master, his job of recording the carts' contents was going to be a struggle on the best of days he was sure.

It took another hour or so before he could sleep and even in his sleep he felt the soft brush of dove's wings.

The morning found his predictions about struggling to keep up a horrible reality. But as the day wore on he developed a system for checking in the carts and also became more familiar and comfortable with the bookkeeping system developed by Philemon. By the time the last of the carts headed back to the fields for the midday meal, he felt he could take time to eat and still not lose his sense of what his master wanted and needed in the records.

The days of the harvest stretched in a seemingly endless stream of sameness as Onesimus counted, recorded and measured the bountiful harvest of a well-run olive grove as others sorted the olives by quality and relegated the crop to the proper presses.

The only breaks in the day came for a shortened mid-day meal. The only breaks in the long lines of carts took place on Lord's Days when the whole household rested. The work was so demanding and the hours so long that he began to anticipate with joy the coming Lord's Day gathering and subsequent rest. Even so, he noticed that on the busiest of days Philemon never quit working until he had dismissed the cart drivers, the sorters, the pressers and Onesimus from their duties.

As Philemon had promised, the meetings began to be familiar in a short time, but they were never boring because there seemed to be no set plan to the gatherings. Sometimes someone would begin a song first, sometimes someone would pray, at other times a letter from Paulus or news from another Apostle would be read first and sometimes someone would ask a question that spurred responses from several people. Onesimus looked forward to hearing and seeing what new things might be said or sung or done by those who gathered at his Master's house.

But even though the days of harvest seemed endless, the final harvest day came at last, and Onesimus felt as if he had passed the whole time in a trance from which he had just awakened.

He knew that as soon as the last of the harvest was pressed and the oil sold and shipped the winter would be close and the cold months might be the most difficult of all to bear. Yet, he was cautiously curious to find out what he would be doing in the winter months.

After the mid-day meal that last day of harvest, while others were busy pressing the many baskets of olives that remained, he seated himself once more at his desk and began to write. When Philemon entered the room, he called out to him.

"Onesimus. I have a need to speak privately with you."

A chill ran down his back as Onesimus recalled the last time he heard that phrase. *How unusual!* He thought. *The master never interrupts work for private conversations.*

Rising from his stool he followed Philemon from the press and out to the yard beyond.

"Onesimus, I am hesitant to bring this to you but I don't know who else could be responsible," Philemon began. "I have found a discrepancy in your books. There seems to be an imbalance of more than fifty sextarii of oil pressed and oil shipped. What happened? I cannot understand how this could be unless someone has stolen a couple of amphorae to sell for themselves."

Onesimus breathed deeply and stared without understanding at the master who had always been so kind. "Are you asking me if I have done such a thing?" He inquired with trembling heart. "Are you *accusing* me of this?" He knew that if Philemon wished, he could have Onesimus flogged, branded or even killed and no one would protest . . . this was the hard reality for those unfortunate enough to be captured or sold into slavery.

Philemon looked troubled and puzzled. He tilted his head to one side as he looked at Onesimus with a concerned frown. "Son, I certainly pray that you did not do this, but if you *did* . . . if you had need of something and wanted money to buy it . . . I could at least feel there was a justification for this betrayal of my trust. If that is the case, please say so now so that we can put this behind us."

Onesimus bowed his head and thought of all his hard work. He had done everything Philemon had asked of him! He hadn't so much as eaten an olive from the carts! And even if he *had* stolen that oil what would it matter to a man as rich as Philemon? But *he hadn't!*

Philemon stood waiting for a reply but all Onesimus could do was shake his head in denial of his involvement in this terrible thing.

"Let me recheck the books, master. I will not protest my innocence until I can solve the riddle of what happened to those jars. But I *will* assure you that there *is* another explanation to this puzzle. *There must be!*" he finally said.

"I so hope you can find that explanation then," Philemon murmured. "I have no wish to find that my trusted servant has betrayed me."

As Onesimus turned and walked back to his desk the gratitude he had felt for the kindness of Philemon began to curdle within his breast and as it did, another emotion... one darker and harsher... began to grow in its place. An emotion he had become mightily familiar with over the last few months and he knew that Paulus called this emotion, *bitterness.*

For three days Onesimus searched his books. He looked for ways that a mathematical mistake may have been made. He looked for ways a shipment might not have been recorded. He looked for ways a count of the vessels of oil could have been wrong. He found nothing... and all the while his resentment and anger toward Philemon grew.

He hadn't done anything wrong! He knew he was innocent, but there was no way he could prove his innocence. His feelings toward Philemon grew hotter as the days went on until he couldn't stand it when the master patted his shoulder... couldn't stand it when the master called him *son,* ... finally he was ready to take the blame and whatever punishment Philemon handed out. He hoped Philemon would grow so frustrated, the punishment would end with Onesimus being sold! *Perhaps,* he thought as he worked, *it would be a very hard beating so that he would die.* He was done being a slave because his father was a wastrel! He'd rather be dead!

As Onesimus was readying himself to approach the master and admit that he couldn't find the problem, Quintin came bursting into the press with excitement dancing in his eyes. He was shouting, "Father! Father! Come see what I found down by Grandfather's cottage!"

Philemon tried to put him off, but the boy insisted that he should come immediately so the two of them started out together.

Now was his chance. It would take the two of them a long time to walk to the grandfather's cottage and back. Onesimus's thoughts raced as he considered his options. He could stay and take the punishment Philemon was certain to impose . . . perhaps even death . . . or he could take what he could get and run! Run as fast and as far as he possibly could! After all, if he was to be beaten for a thief he might as well *act* like a thief! Run all the way to Rome where he could get lost among the throngs of senators and visitors, citizens and Plebians. He knew where Philemon kept his purse filled with plenty of money for the trip. No doubt enough money to buy passage on a ship headed to Rome. He hesitated a short moment. Philemon had always been a fair and gentle master . . . but then, Onesimus had given him no reason to be other than fair and gentle! Now Philemon had a reason (albeit a false one) and Onesimus had no doubt he would find his master to be as harsh in his judgments as he had been with his own servants before his fall from "beloved son" to "for sale".

The other workers saw nothing awry as he crossed the pressing house to Philemon's desk. Opening the door of the storage area he reached in and grasped the kidskin bag and hefted it. YES! There was plenty of money here.

Without another thought, Onesimus went quickly to the door and through it running for the orchard across the road and then down toward the brook. From there, he walked in a generally westerly direction knowing that sooner or later he would come to Ephesus where he could book passage for Rome.

CHAPTER EIGHT

Onesimus had walked from Colossae through groves and fields, avoiding roads for fear of being caught, always heading westward. He'd slept in the open the first night and that hadn't been too bad. The stars overhead and the slight breeze brushing his face made him almost glad he'd done this foolish thing.

The next day saw him up and traveling as the sun came up. His stomach growled, complaining about the lack of food and Onesimus remembered a saying his best friend used when he was very hungry, "My backbone's going to rub a hole in my belly if I don't eat soon!"

By midday, he was so hungry he took up a station behind a large bush and watched the road, hoping a traveler would come along that would be willing to sell him a little food. He saw one cart and was almost ready to step out and signal it when he recognized the driver as one of Philemon's slaves. Ducking quickly back behind his bush, he waited for another chance. He was almost ready to give up hope and melt back into the woods when he saw a man walking along the road. The man was so fat he waddled more than walked and he carried in his hand a small stick with which he urged his loaded donkey along. The man's efforts weren't in the least cruel, simply a little poke in the rump and the balky burro would start moving again. As he walked, the man hummed a little tune that Onesimus thought was rather pleasant although a little flat.

Gathering his courage, Onesimus stepped onto the road and hailed the man, "Kind sir! Excuse me but I've been trying to reach my dying brother. When I heard, I left in such a hurry I didn't even consider how I would eat along the way. Have you anything you could spare? I will gladly pay you for it."

The man's eyes narrowed as he peered at Onesimus closely. Onesimus stood and endured the searching gaze for what seemed like several minutes until the man spoke. "Aye, friend, 'tis a sad thing to see your brother die! Never mind the coin! I'm not a rich man but I won't begrudge a piece of cheese to a man who is anticipating a close visit from the thief of souls!"

Onesimus gladly reached into the donkey's pack and drew out a chunk of cheese. The man gestured toward the pack a second time, "Here now, that tisn't enough to sustain ye! Help yerself to a loaf as well!"

About sunset, it began raining and a cold wind started to blow. The runaway decided he had to find shelter in an abandoned house. That night he became closely acquainted with Brother Rat and Sister Beetle. With no cloak to wrap in and no padding to sleep on the night was a long one, indeed! Thinking about his stool and his desk, being able to sit still for a while, having shelter and decent food, his own couch to sleep on and a warm coverlet to wrap in, he considered turning around and going back. Just as quickly though he realized he had done too much damage and so he would continue for a little while until the gods gave him some omen about what he should do.

Thinking back upon the omen of the dove landing on his foot, he no longer thought it had been an omen for good. No. It had, of a fact, been an omen for evil! If not, why was he here, alone on the road, tired to the bone, hungry, and cold?

It was the morning of the third day when he saw before him a small hamlet of about seventy people. Most of them seemed to be in the town square, gathered around something that was arousing strong feelings in the throng. He wandered closer to the crowd until he could hear the screams of someone buried at the center of the gathering. He tapped one of the villagers on the shoulder.

"What's happening? Why is that man screaming?"

"Caught us a runaway, now didn't we?" came the reply. "Master's been lookin' for him for about a week now. Seems he's been hiding right here in our town most of that time! Well, he won't be running away again, I'd say! An' I doubt if any slave of his acquaintance will try to hide out in our town, either!"

Onesimus was about to ask why when the answer landed at his feet. The slave, shoved through the crowd, fell squarely in front of Onesimus. The runaway, sobbing and shaking, looked up at Onesimus and there, on his forehead, a new brand was burned into his skin. It was the letter R... for Runaway.

Well, I've certainly been given a clear omen now! Onesimus thought wryly. No going back.

Thanks to the treatment he had received at Philemon's hand, he had decent clothing and sound sandals. No one could look at him and recognize him as a runaway slave. He was safe enough for a short stay . . . long enough to purchase a cloak, some bread and cheese and a small flagon of wine. Then he was off again, heading west, moving off the road and into the surrounding fields and, after a time, sitting on the ground and leaning against a low stone wall he found along his way.

After a short break he stood up and headed out . . . always west . . . hoping to reach Ephesus where he could book passage on a Rome-bound ship.

It was almost sunset when he came upon a wood that seemed somehow different. It was darker. And damp. And eerily quiet. He heard no birds or rustle of underbrush. He hesitated before he plunged into the trees.

The rain from the night before hadn't seemed to penetrate the overarching branches and the ground remained quite dry. It would be a good place to spend the night . . . it really would . . . but just as the rain didn't penetrate, neither did any light. As the shadows of the great trees lengthened and night came on, even the light that entered from the edge of the forest faded and disappeared. Onesimus had only moved a short distance into the trees when he realized that, to travel any farther, he would have to travel with one hand outstretched to keep from running into the black, rough tree trunks that surrounded him. It was almost with a sense of relief that he turned back to the spot where he had entered and wrapped up in his new cloak just inside the edge of the forest, where it was dry enough and he could still discern a little light.

Travel through the fields and forests instead of the road ensured that his going would be slow and he would cover much less than the average of twenty miles a day. It was the afternoon of the eighth day before his journey brought him into the region surrounding his goal. Although two Lord's Days had passed, he had not rested since his sudden flight, traveling right through them. Just the day before he had skirted a town called Magnesia and he could tell he was getting close by the increased traffic on the road as he approached the town. Crowds of people passed him by walking, men in carts brought goods to market, and women, some carrying offerings for the gods and some herding children with sharp shouts and quick hands on disobedient rumps. All seemed to welcome him to this unfamiliar but famous city.

His one fear was that as he neared the city itself he might run into some of the Master's carters, taking a rest after hauling the last of the harvest's oil to the great ships moored there.

Despite the blisters on his heels, he quickened his pace and moved forward, all the while fingering the kidskin bag he'd tucked inside his clothing.

By mid-afternoon he topped a rise and suddenly below him lay the city of Ephesus. It sprawled out like a brazen woman and stretched its arms around the harbor where Onesimus could see the masts of several ships. And, like a brazen woman, the coastal city teemed with temptations and allurements that a wise young man like Onesimus would do his best to avoid.

Spying a fallen tree not too far off the road, Onesimus seated himself on it facing the city with its great harbor on its far western side. He watched the ships move gently with the sea. The rest was welcome and now that he was within sight of his goal, he decided to take his time and enjoy the final afternoon of his walking travels.

Shortly, Onesimus became aware of an aroma he hadn't smelled for more than a week. The smell of fresh-baked *panis rusticus,* a bran bread, was wafting from the open windows of a small cottage he hadn't even noticed.

The cottage sat back from the road behind a thicket of brambles. It was a humble home and Onesimus was certain that if the owners became aware of the gold he carried they might very well succumb to temptation and relieve him of it. But his mouth was watering in anticipation of something crusty and warm and he had some smaller coins as well that had been given to him as change for a small purchase earlier. He fished a couple of these from his bag.

He rounded the end of the thorny thicket and approached the front of the cottage.

Before he'd crossed the garden plot he found himself in, the front door opened and a woman about his own age or slightly older emerged.

"Hello, weary traveler!" she called out and her voice was like a bell with a crack in it. It was a beautiful voice but with an undercurrent of hoarseness that detracted from the melody of her speech. "Are you seeking only a place to rest or are you as hungry as you look?"

"Mistress," he replied as he tried to sound casual. "I am indeed in search of a place to rest for a short time and also I am hungry. I was hoping I could purchase from you a bit of that wonderful bread I smell."

She smiled widely and replied, "Under no circumstances may you purchase any of my bread."

He started to break in, "But I am willing to . . ."

"You may not purchase it but you are welcome to share a loaf with us along with a bit of lamb left over from supper last night and some decent wine besides," she continued with an unwavering smile.

Onesimus was taken aback to hear that the meal would consist of much more than bread and cheese or eggs. How unusual that people who lived in this small cabin would have meat to eat! "Thank you so much, mistress! I've been traveling and would certainly appreciate a meal, but I must insist on paying for it," he said firmly.

"Nonsense! The God we serve would not want us to take money for a small repast given to a wayfarer. Please come in and meet my husband."

She stepped aside and bade him enter where he saw seated at a table a roughhewn man in his mid-twenties. The man had a grin on his face so large it seemed the room could not contain it. He motioned the traveler in and offered him a seat on the bench beside himself.

"Hello!" he spoke almost entirely in exclamations. "Here! Sit by me and enjoy the finest food in the region prepared by my own wife, Faith!"

His voice was surprisingly high pitched for a man of his size and Onesimus was slightly taken aback by it. "Oh yes!" the man continued. "Kiffien is my name and welcome to my home! And what are YOU called?"

Onesimus responded carefully, knowing he couldn't use his own name, "Zacheus, son of Simeon." It was the name of a boyhood friend.

The food was already on the table and Faith joined them without hesitation.

As Onesimus started to reach for the delicious-looking lamb, Kiffien's work roughened hand reached out and grasped his. Onesimus jumped, concerned that somehow this Kiffien had discerned the presence of gold. But in the next moment Kiffien reached with his right hand and took Faith's left hand, who reached her right hand across the table to clasp Onesimus' left one.

Onesimus had been in Philemon's house long enough to realize that followers of Philemon's God often clasped hands this way to pray so he sat respectfully as his hosts' heads bowed and they gave thanks for the food on the table, the lovely day and their new friend.

"I take it you're not of the Way," Kiffien said when he had finished and Onesimus' plate was full.

"No sir, I'm not . . . but I know the Way whereof you speak. I spent several months . . ." Onesimus suddenly realized that he could not divulge the truth of where he'd learned of the Way. Then he continued, "I spent several months with a cousin in Pergamum who follows the Way."

Kiffien tilted his head to one side and nodded slightly. "Yes. I see." Faith asked, "So husband, did you find a buyer for that old nanny? I must admit I'm glad she's gone! I was getting mightily tired of catching her with my best linens half eaten! How *ever* she managed to escape her pen every laundry day I will never be able to fathom!"

"Ah, my dearest!" Kiffien replied with a laugh, "I do not know how she found her way to your washing, but I know I would gladly jump a fence to gain access to anything edible you prepared for me!"

Faith gave a small laugh. "Oh, but while you might consider many things edible that less hungry men would not, I doubt if you would include cleaning cloths and togas on your menu of choice!"

Kiffien turned toward Onesimus. "What do you think, Zacheus? Would togas be a suitable item on the dinner table?"

Onesimus smiled and shook his head, "I wouldn't think so, but after the last few days I might find it acceptable."

"Long journeys often bring on that attitude in a man!" Kiffien rejoined.

After a slight pause that made Onesimus a touch nervous, Kiffien, having noticed that his guest had devoured the bread, lamb and wine that had been served to him said, "Have some more warm bread!"

Onesimus gladly obeyed the command and succeeded in eating himself drowsy.

A few minutes later, Kiffien saw Onesimus' head bob for the third time. "Faith," Kiffien said quietly. "It seems our new friend is exhausted. Let's help him to a pallet and let him sleep."

Chapter Nine

Even through his closed eyelids Onesimus could tell the sun was shining brightly because he saw before him a wall of red. He raised his arm and dropped his forearm over his eyes before he opened them.

"Well, Slug-a-bed!" Came the melodious scratch of his hostess's voice. "I see you've decided to return from your slumbers at last. Kiffien is already gone for the day and I am half-done with breakfast clean-up but you're welcome to fresh milk from our nanny and some of yesterday's bread."

Onesimus half sat up dropping his arm from his face to prop himself against it. "How long?" he asked groggily.

"Well, you dropped off before you even finished your supper and it's now nearly through the morning so . . .," she replied.

"I am so sorry!" he exclaimed. He jumped up and took the broom from Faith's hands. "Let me at least sweep your floors to thank you for that fine meal"

Faith took the broom back and smiled warmly. "You are our guest and guests do NOT do housework. Please help yourself to some milk and bread and have a seat."

"Milk from the nanny Kiffien sold?"

Faith laughed. "No. We had two nannies!"

Onesimus took her up on her offer and sat dipping the crusty bread in warm goat's milk.

"I must be going after I've helped you clean up," he said. "I've been traveling for many days and yet my journey is only beginning."

Faith nodded and spoke quietly, "Your journey has only begun in many ways, Zacheus." As Onesimus finished his simple breakfast she continued, "There is no cleaning left to do. Just rinse your vessel and we shall pray before you leave."

He did as she asked and then she placed her hand on his arm and bowed her head.

"Father of creation, I exalt Your name over all. I surrender to your mercies all I am and all I have. Great God I ask that you go with Zacheus on his journey. Help him to find what he is searching for and help him to come to the Way. Protect him as he travels and guide him safely to your harbor.

"Thank you, Father. Amen."

The simple but heartfelt prayer touched something deep in Onesimus and set his heartstrings vibrating. He opened his mouth to speak but then closed it again. After months in the home of Philemon, he knew that Faith prayed to the only God who was real... and yet he could not... *would* not surrender his will.

Instead, he simply looked at Faith and said, "Thank you. I am certain your God heard your prayer for me and will grant your requests." He stepped over the threshold as Faith smiled and waved him on his way.

He wondered if the prayer would count for him since she prayed for "Zacheus" ... did her God know anyone named Zacheus that might get the blessings Faith prayed for him? Would the answer to her prayer be sent to a real Zacheus or to him? He hoped it would come to him.

As he made his way down the road toward the great Temple of Artemis he saw that most of the travelers on the road with him were moving onto the temple grounds. Even so, his curiosity wasn't truly piqued until he had passed the entrance himself. Many women in gauzy, see-through clothing at the entrance tried to entice him in with promises of great blessings from the fertility goddess after an *offering* to her temple prostitutes was made. Since Onesimus neither wanted a blessing from Artemis nor a union with any of these potentially diseased women, he declined firmly and continued on his journey.

It took him until midafternoon to make his way through the city and down to the harbor. When he got there he was greatly discouraged to see there were no ships preparing to sail. The ships he had seen in the harbor the day before lay at anchor and the ships at the docks had no activity at all around them.

He closed his eyes and shook his head. He couldn't believe that he had come all this way and missed the last of the sailing season! It was right there in front of him every day. He knew the season for storms was coming and he knew the last of the olive harvest wouldn't be shipped until spring. All this He knew and still he had decided to run away with no place to go! Now what would he do? Should he set off on foot for part of the journey? Or should he just wait out the winter and sail in the spring? He didn't know and he needed time to think, so he headed back toward town, hoping to find a place to spend a few days where he could decide what to do.

As Onesimus left the docks and moved toward the town. He really wasn't aware of his surroundings as he walked. His mind was occupied by his plan for the next three or four months when shipping resumed. He must have wandered in the right direction because it wasn't long before he was surrounded by a host of people. The crowd brought him back to reality and he realized he was standing in the marketplace.

A solid *thump!* struck him in the back as he stopped dead in his tracks.

"Here! Ya can't stop in the middle of the street like that!" an angry female voice shouted behind him. "Ya gotta give some warning!"

Onesimus turned and looked at the speaker in surprise. "I'm sorry. I didn't mean to cause a problem. I was wrapped up in my circumstances instead of paying attention. I was planning on sailing today for Rome but I discovered that I had missed the last sailing vessel of the season!

"Now, I have nowhere to stay and I am at a loss for what to do. Do you know of a place I could winter?"

The woman, a skinny little thing about one-and-a-third meters tall, put her hands up to her tip-tilted hairdo and gave it a mighty shove then looked up at him and smiled. "Indeed I do! I have some repairs I need done on my house and since my husband died these three years ago, there has been no one to help me. I will gladly give you a cot if you can fix things up for me!"

A smile spread across Onesimus' face. "That would be wonderful! We both benefit from the arrangement and I will be able to sail in the spring!"

"My name is Philomena," the woman informed him. "Follow me through the market and you can carry my purchases for me, but mind you don't run off with 'em! I have friends that would hunt you down in a trice!"

Onesimus hid his smirk, thinking to himself, *from formal slave to practical slave... well, at least there is an end in sight!* Then he had to fight the urge to suggest that, if she had so many friends, couldn't one of them loan her a husband for a few days to do the repairs? That *certainly* wouldn't be smart since he needed the lodging!

Philomena, it turned out was the widow of a well-to-do merchant who had left her well off, indeed. Her home was located just a short distance from the marketplace where she had literally run into Onesimus. This was where her husband had traded. It was where he had built enough of a fortune that his widow would never have to worry about money; although she had no idea how to acquire the help she needed to keep her home in good repair.

She informed Onesimus she had been barren and had suffered great indignities at the hands of her late husband because of it. Therefore, she wasn't terribly grieved over his passing.

After they had arrived at her home, Philomena showed Onesimus a straw-filled mat near the back of the house where he could bed down. She also offered him a tunic that had belonged to her late husband.

She told Onesimus that the first thing that needed doing was the replacement of some tiles on the floor of the salon. He spoke with bravado, telling her that he had helped tile many floors and knew what he was doing. But when he saw the intricate details of the tiling, the mosaic pattern of light and dark tiles, he hesitated to begin. Even so, begin he did and did a fairly good job of replacing an area of broken tiles about one meter square. A task that, in the end, only took about a week to complete.

Next came six broken balusters in the staircases of the house. Each one had been carved with a somewhat intricate pattern of laurel leaves and Philomena explained that her late husband had enjoyed wood carving and had carved the spindles himself. Then she dug out her husband's box of artisan's wood chisels and told him to take his time and copy the pattern as best he could. If he couldn't get anything more done than those spindles during his stay that would be compensation enough for his room and board she assured him.

At first, Onesimus was overwhelmed with the idea of carving spindles and had to battle his own sense of inadequacy, but it wasn't long before he felt confident in the craft and even realized that he was getting good at carving. From that point on, he drew the pattern with care onto each spindle and then carved every one with pride. After each spindle was completed, he would smooth it carefully until it was satiny to the touch. Next came staining them with approximately the same color as the originals. Then he exchanged each broken one with his replacement. Each spindle took about ten days to complete, so he estimated that this particular task would take him almost until time to sail in the spring.

When the final spindle had been replaced, Philomena was so happy with his work that she threw a party and invited many of her friends to attend. She greeted each guest, as was the custom, with a kiss on each cheek. When they had all arrived, she led the group into the salon to show off her new floor and then to the staircases to show off her newly carved balusters. She called Onesimus in from the kitchen. Taking him by the arm, she spoke to her guests. "Zacheus has been sent to me by the gods, I do declare! I ran into him, really ran into him, in the marketplace last fall. He had missed his chance to sail for Rome and I was in need of some repair work. He needed a place to stay and he has been trading board and room here for doing this beautiful work!

"It is a shame that his time with me is coming to an end."

Onesimus's heart leaped in his chest. Was it true? Had the season of storms ended? When were the ships beginning to sail?

"Zacheus, I heard yesterday that a ship will be leaving for Rome in a fortnight. I know how anxious you are to finish your journey, and yet I almost didn't tell you because I would like to keep you here. Nevertheless, I thought it only fair that I deal with you honestly and let you know about the ship."

The ever-present stack of hair on her head began to tip again and she absently reached up to push it back into place.

Onesimus fought to maintain a straight face and a calm exterior as he nodded and thanked Philomena for the information. He knew it would be all he could manage to stay away from the docks until it was time to sail and yet, he would miss the tiny Philomena with her tipsy hair and her sweetly imperious ways.

CHAPTER TEN

Onesimus shouldered his way through the crowd and grabbed the elbow of a passing sailor. "Can you tell me of a ship that is sailing for Rome?" he asked over the din.

The sailor frowned, glancing first at the hand on his arm and then up at the man who had stopped him. "Here! I'm just starting a month-long voyage and I've no time to talk to you! Go ask over there!" and he pointed at a short, round man who was standing in the middle of a small crowd.

Onesimus thanked the man and moved toward the crowd but it wasn't long before a thought came into his head that made him pause. It would not be smart to remove his purse from his shirt and take gold from it in the presence of people he not only did not know, but with whom he would be isolated aboard a ship for several days at least. Someone shoved a sharp elbow in his side. As he passed out of the harbor area a woman of middle years, and certain occupation, sidled up to him and offered him things he had no intention of taking part in. Her state of undress was enough to inform him of all she was and all she had been.

He found a quiet corner, sheltered on three sides by crates and boxes and stepped into the open side. Facing the wall of crates, he reached inside his shirt and removed from his purse several gold coins. Then tucked the purse back inside his shirt and moved back toward the harbor and the man who had been indicated by the sailor.

As he came closer he could hear the man in the middle shouting and could see him pointing, "Crete!" he would shout and point at one of the ships. "Athens!" another ship would be designated. "Alexandria!" a third ship would be targeted by his pointing finger. "Thessalonica!"

"Excuse me!" Onesimus shouted to be heard. "I need to go to Rome. Which . . .?"

The man glanced up with a frown, shook his head as if to say *What fool doesn't know which destination takes him closer to Rome?* But he just said, "PUTEOLI!" and pointed at a two-masted ship lying at anchor at one of the larger docks.

The ship, The Swan, out of Alexandria, had the twin gods Castor and Pollux as its protectors and was taking on cargo. It looked as if the vessel was almost loaded and Onesimus knew he'd have to hurry if he were to have a chance to purchase passage. So he hurried down the wharf and up the gangplank.

A man about Onesimus's height but weighing only about half as much was overseeing the loading of cargo. Onesimus waited a few minutes until there was a momentary lull. Then he spoke up, "Excuse me, I need to book passage to Rome. Can you . . .?"

The man looked him up and down and replied not unkindly.

"The Captain is aboard. He's up there," he pointed at the bow of the ship. "Why don't you go ask him about it? I'm sure we can take you on."

Onesimus hurried forward and asked after the Captain once again.

"Tha's him right there!" a rough-looking boy of about thirteen told him.

Onesimus doubted if the boy had had any sort of wash-up in the last year or so, but thanked him and moved onward.

Approaching the Captain, Onesimus watched as he directed crewmen this way and that, shouting encouragement to someone doing it right and rebukes to someone doing it wrong.

"Here now!" he shouted. "Fausines! You got that amphora almost upside down! Right that right now before I keelhaul ye!"

The Captain looked up at him and Onesimus stepped forward.

"Sir, I'd like to know how I can book passage to Rome," he said.

"Captain Alban!" the Captain replied. "Well, sir! Welcome to the Swan under the protection of Castor and Pollux. We're going to Puteoli, that's the port Rome uses, about nine days' walk from Rome, with stops in Crete and Sicily and we've an empty berth you can buy or we can always..." here he looked at a passing sailor who slouched by with indifference, "MAKE ROOM FOR YOU ON OUR CREW!"

The sailor glanced over his shoulder at the Captain and straightened up, hurrying to do his duty before his was the room that was made.

Onesimus and Captain Alban grinned at each other.

"That won't be necessary," Onesimus said. "I've got the money right here."

With that he handed the Captain several gold pieces. The Captain, cautious man that he was, lifted one of the gold coins to his mouth and bit it between the four teeth he still possessed. Satisfied that they were genuine, Captain Alban shook Onesimus' hand and directed him to a berth.

The following morning the ship left harbor with the tide and moved out into the Great Sea on the first leg of its voyage.

Onesimus stood on deck, wondering what had gotten into him and why he had gotten himself into this horrible maze of wrong turns.

These same thoughts had been wandering round and round in his brain since last November on the second night of his run. The night he had had to make friends with rats, lizards, snakes and bugs in an abandoned hovel where he'd sought what little shelter he could find from the cold rain.

After a while, with the deck rocking beneath his feet and the masts creaking he became more aware of his surroundings. He heard the distant cry of gulls and the nearby luffing of the sails as the ship turned too close into the wind. He saw the helmsman hurry to correct the problem and watched as the wind filled them again and began to push the ship through the waves. At that point he wondered if perhaps he could learn seamanship and become a sailor. He was beginning to enjoy the freedom he felt as the ship glided through the water ahead of the warm, salt-laden breeze.

He smelled the salt tang of the tide and licked his lips. He wasn't surprised to find his lips had taken on the saltiness of the surrounding sea. The rough wooden rail he rested his hands on suddenly seemed to be no more substantial than the netting the sailors used to climb the masts.

While the sailors shouted to one another Captain Alban was shouting commands. It seemed as if no one could possibly hear what was supposed to be done, but somehow all the work was quickly completed.

"Crete's the first stop. We've a load of wheat to unload and we'll pick up some fine pottery for the Roman markets there. It will take about four days in Fair Havens to offload and reload," Captain Alban's voice came over his right shoulder. "Then it's on to Sicily to take on some dyes and furniture and to offload some small items ordered by a rich widow who will, as always, meet the ship at the docks and pay with gold for her cargo.

"When we leave the Sicilian harbor you can know that Puteoli is our next port of call."

Onesimus simply nodded his understanding and continued to look out over the bow before answering.

"Then it should be a fairly simple voyage, shouldn't it? The season for storms is over?"

Alban clapped him on the back and laughed, "Yes! The stormy season is past and there should be an easy sail ahead of us. Rest easy. You will be safe on the shores of Puteoli long before there is any need to lash yourself to the mast... unless you aren't!" the captain said with a wink.

CHAPTER ELEVEN

The long, narrow island of Crete offered almost any type of scenery one could wish for. The hills and countryside presented a beauty especially appealing to one who had spent time on the open sea. Someone wandering far enough inland could find mountains, plains and even a high desert.

On its way to the port of Lasea, the ship passed an arm of the island that had huge rocks tumbled about in the water. Some of them had been eroded by the tides into fantastical shapes as they stood in the ocean shallows. Onesimus and several off-duty crew members amused themselves commenting on the odd shapes they saw in the rocks just as children comment on the clouds. One he saw he thought was shaped like a mermaid and another one seemed to be a horse rearing up on its hind legs. One of the crewmen argued that it looked more like a bear getting ready to attack.

"And of course, you being a man of the sea would know *exactly* what a bear of the woods looks like when he is getting ready to attack!" Onesimus laughed.

Within the span of half a day of that sighting, the ship docked at the Lasea port. The Romans, when they conquered Minoa and Crete, declared the town of Gorton to be Crete's capital city. Even so, Lasea was a common seaport for sailing ships bound for Italy, Cyprus, or Asia. The port was bustling with activity and its buildings came down almost to the docks, with mountains rising in the distance behind them.

While the ship was offloading its Cretan cargo and taking on the carefully packed pottery they were taking on to Puteoli, Onesimus grabbed the chance to walk on solid ground for the few days the Swan would be moored. Everyone he met was smiling and friendly and it wasn't long before he had relaxed his guard enough to smile back. Wandering through the stone-paved streets of the city, Onesimus thought that if Crete had been a little further from Colossae he might very well have been content to make his home there instead of traveling on to Rome. His thoughts were cut short, however, when a young woman ran up to him and grasped him firmly by the arm.

"I see you!" she whispered conspiratorially. "I know you. I know your past, I know your future! Your future is full of joy and sorrow, fulfillment and want! And your past... Your *past...is...*"

Onesimus shook her off his arm as he raised his fist threateningly. "You know *nothing* of my future and even *less* about my past! Leave me woman before I show you that you don't even know your *own* future!"

She pulled back and hurried away while Onesimus stood there watching and wondering what ever had made him react like that. Soothsayers weren't an unfamiliar sight on the city streets so he hadn't been surprised to be accosted. Could it have been fear that, perhaps ... just perhaps ... the woman *could* see his past!?!

Onesimus traveled further away from the port and into the countryside and as he did, he became aware of a sweet but subtle aroma that permeated the air. Was it some sort of flower? He knew it must be something quite plentiful to actually scent the air all around. When he topped the rise in the road he had his conjectures confirmed. Off to his left he saw a large field covered with spiky, light purple flowers that looked almost more like shrubs than flowering plants. He stood there in the middle of the road and inhaled deeply, enjoying the odor and the sight of the field of lavender.

After a short rest on a nearby rock, breathing in the wonderful scent, he stood and turned with a sigh, reluctantly made his way back to the town. He would spend the nights on the ship and the next two or three days wandering the island. The unloading and loading of the ship was set to take three days and when it was loaded, the ship would be leaving on the next tide.

It was three days exactly when he again found himself leaning on the railing of the outward bound ship. The only difference was that this time, he knew a little more of what he could expect over the next few days. Onesimus was savoring the last few bites of a pair of figs he had purchased on the way back to the ship when the captain moved up beside him.

"Well, my young friend, the port of Syracuse on the island of Sicily is next. It's also the last stop before we reach the port of Puteoli where you will leave us. Syracuse is also where we gain a little gold for a little cargo," he paused thoughtfully. "All in all, not a bad trade!"

"Is Sicily much like Crete?" Onesimus asked. "I thought Crete was so beautiful I almost stayed there, but I really must get on to Rome."

Alban gave a hearty laugh, "An island is an island, son! At least those islands that make their dwelling in Our Sea are all much alike.

"I've heard tales from other sailors, though, that would turn your hair gray and curl your beard! Why, one friend of mine, who has sailed between the Pillars of Hercules, told me there's an isle just beyond the Pillars where fantastical creatures live. There are men there who walk upright on the legs of goats and women who have three breasts instead of two. Hidden away in a cave on that island is a whole family of bears with one eye each and teeth as long and sharp as a Centurion's longsword! The worst thing we can boast here in Our Sea is the island where the Sirens dwell and lure the unwary sailors to their deaths on the rocks!"

"Here, Sailor!" Alban shouted at a crewmember who was supposed to be ordering the sheets but instead was tangling them almost beyond hope. "Order those sheets aright or you'll find yourself waving good voyage to the Swan and all her crew from the wharf at Syracuse!"

He shook his head and turned back to Onesimus. "You may as well settle in for a while. We will be sailing into deep waters where storms abound and the sweet song of the Sirens I've told you of can drive a man to his ruin!"

90

"You're certain it isn't the season for storms?" Onesimus asked uneasily.

Alban just patted the runaway on his shoulder and shook his head. "Whenever there is a storm it's the season for storms, boy! While there are more storms at some seasons of the year than at others there isn't a day in the calendar that hasn't seen at least one horrible blow in the last hundred years. No matter though, this here is the finest crew I've ever sailed with and we will bring you safe to Sicily and to the Italian coast, never fear."

It was the next day, after the coastline had receded into the distance and there was nothing to see but water in every direction, that Onesimus had reason to pray that Captain Alban's promise hadn't been simply idle boasting.

The storm struck before dawn. The night watch called the men who had just turned in as well as those who had begun to rouse for the day. It was immediately clear to all on board that the pitch and roll of the ship had changed dramatically. Even Onesimus could tell the difference and the sailors immediately left their other duties to grab some of the hardtack that was on hand for just such emergencies and cram some in their mouths and some inside their sashes or shirts to save for later in the day.

The Captain was shouting orders and making certain that everything was secured for the coming blow as some of his crew worked in the hold checking for loose cargo as well as slack ropes and chains. Others were securing the sails, lashing the ship with ropes to add a little extra support to the hull and battening down the hatch lids. Onesimus wanted to offer his help, but Captain Alban warned Onesimus that he needed to get below deck and stay there for the duration. A storm was no place for a landlubber to learn seafaring. He also suggested that some hardtack might come in handy because it might be several days before the blow was over.

Knowing that experience brought wisdom, the runaway took to heart what Captain Alban said and retreated to his hammock with a couple fistfuls of the tough unleavened bread that could satisfy his hunger and sustain him for several days.

By the end of the second day of listening to the wild keening of the wind and riding the violent bucking of the ship through the swells, Onesimus was certain he would never see Syracuse let alone Rome and he wondered if the dream he'd had about being in a shipwreck and clinging to a board with his brother and father had been a warning. Fear filled his heart as he realized he wasn't ready to die. He knew deep within his breast that the God of Philemon was real but still he was afraid to approach him. He had treated Philemon so badly and he thought he could never win the favor of a God whose faithful follower had been as badly wronged as he had wronged Philemon.

By the morning of the third day, he was rolling around in his hammock convinced he would never eat again. He had discovered to his great chagrin that even if he managed to learn sea-craft he would only be able to sail on sunny days. The pitching and rolling had rocked not only the ship stem to stern and starboard to port but it had also rocked his belly, and his belly had given up holding onto *anything* until the storm was history.

It was about midday when Onesimus was shot out of his bunk by an earsplitting *CRACK!* and the crew, as if in unision, gave up a tremendous shout.

Convinced his dream of shipwreck was coming true he flew up the ladder onto the deck. There he found the crew and the captain all fighting to stay on their feet, cursing using words Onesimus thought he might never have heard before and struggling to detangle the sheets and jettison the forward mast which had snapped as one would snap a twig. It was lying across the bow of the boat causing the boat to wallow in the troughs of the waves even more than it had been.

Onesimus rushed to help create a fulcrum out of the stump of the mast and lever the ungainly beam over the side of the ship.

When the job was finished, Captain Alban gave him a nod and just said, "Good man!"

Onesimus' heart filled with pride as he realized the captain had paid him a finer tribute than his father ever had. He retreated to his bunk where he lay playing those two words over and over in his head, "Good man! Good man! Good man!" as he drifted off to sleep.

He was awakened by something he couldn't quite put his finger on. Something was different. He shook his head and tried to place the change.

Of course! The wind had died down and the ship was scudding gently along ahead of a fair following sea and making fine use of a breeze that was filling the remaining sail with speed.

Climbing the ladder, he found that most of the crew had disappeared.

Having fought the storm valiantly for the last three–or was it four?—days, they had left their posts within minutes of the breaking of the storm and had retreated to their bunks to recover from their exhaustion. Unlike Onesimus, they weren't interested in how blue the sky now was nor how sweet smelling was the fresh zephyr that was pushing them ever onward toward their destination. So Onesimus lay down on a hatch cover and breathed deeply until he began to relax and let the tension of the last few days drain from him and shortly he, too, slept.

CHAPTER TWELVE

L and!" the shout rang out from the crow's nest. "Land ho! To the nor'west!"

Onesimus had been occupying himself by watching a couple of sailors splicing lines. He had even tried his own hand at it but when the welcome call rang out both he and the sailors stopped what they were doing and lifted their heads.

The lookout was pointing to the northwest and everyone's eyes followed his directing finger and strained to see the welcome sight of land. There! A dark smudge between sky and sea lay on the far horizon. As if in confirmation of the lookout's shout, the air suddenly was filled with the cries of sea gulls looking for a handout. Wings crowded the sky and the mariners' ears filled with the whiffling of wind through feathers. Onesimus laughed when he saw one brave gull alight on the deck railing right in front of one of the toughest of the tough sailors who looked around to see if anyone was watching and, reassured, grinned widely and tossed a bit of hardtack to the deck for the hungry little beggar.

Even with the sighting of land there was another day's sailing before they reached the island of Sicily, and for the crew another day of hard toil. By the time they had finally dropped anchor and gotten ashore, Onesimus was grateful to find that the ship was going to be in port for three days while they took on more provisions and awaited the arrival of the rich widow. She had waited in port for the storm-delayed ship until the day before but had finally given up her vigil and returned to her home leaving a slave to come after her as soon as the ship arrived or news came that it had been lost.

As he wandered the streets of Syracuse he spied several inns and, deciding he wanted to spend his three nights in port in a bed that didn't rock, he looked them over carefully and chose one far from the harbor where he could opt to pay for a pallet to himself or share one with strangers. With a sufficient supply of Philemon's money still in his purse, he chose to sleep alone.

The next day it seemed to Onesimus that the streets were full of the story of a ship that had run aground and had been broken up off the island of Malta during a blow in one of the last voyages of the previous autumn.

Fanciful tales were being told of a man from that ship who had been bitten by a viper and simply shook the deadly serpent off into the fire. According to the accounts the man never even sickened from the bite! Some insisted this man must be a god, for who else could survive such a thing?

It was revealed that the captain of the ship had wanted to take to the lifeboats during the storm but this man/god had insisted that all would be lost if they abandoned the ship. When he gave his word that if the crew remained on the ship not a man would be lost, the captain was persuaded to remain with the boat. Why the captain believed such an unbelievable promise coming from a landlubber no one could explain, but he did believe and the man/god proved to be absolutely right.

The crew and passengers of that ship had made it to the shores of Malta after the wreck and spent some time sheltering with Publius, the chief official of the island who owned a nearby estate.

There was a great stir when the man who had been bitten healed Publius' father of fever and dysentery. When word got out, many Maltese came to him to be healed of all sorts of things. It was three months after the storm when the men who had been aboard that ill-fated ship were finally able to head for Syracuse and even later, Puteoli, where they would start their nine day journey overland to Rome.

Curious about this god/man, Onesimus wandered the streets asking fellow travelers about the man and listening for any news of where he had gone or what he was doing now.

There wasn't very much information he hadn't heard in the first few reports, but some facts emerged through his close questioning of a local fisherman about the events.

Onesimus came upon the man while he was bent over his nets mending them.

"Tell me my friend," Onesimus started. "Have you heard about the man who shook off a viper and survived?"

The fisherman squinted against the sun as he looked up from his task.

"Aye! I've not only heard of him, I met him and talked with him."

"There must be some other explanation, though. It must have been a harmless snake, right?" Onesimus continued.

"No! 'twere a viper all right. I met both the man himself and the Roman guard who was taking him and several other prisoners to Rome and both told me it were a viper... no doubt!" The man placed one hand on his back and straightened up with a slight groan.

"The man's name was Paulus. He is a Roman citizen who got into trouble with the Jews for teaching some doctrine that made 'em mad... teachin' it in their own TEMPLE!" The fisherman gave a short laugh. "He appealed to Caesar and so was on his way to his trial when the ship, out of Adramyttium, I believe, ran aground and broke up. He was part of some new cult. Something called... let me see, now... OH! Aye! He said he was a "Christian" not a god... that he followed the one and only true God. And that god's name was Yeshua! A god with a Jewish name, no less!" The fisherman shook his head with amusement, unaware of the effect his words had on Onesimus who could only stand there and wait for his heart to stop hammering and his breath to return to his lungs.

"One more thing, friend," he said, when he was finally able to create sound again. "Where is this man now?"

"Probably dead!" came the quick reply. "He was on his way to trial before Caesar so if he's NOT dead he's probably somewhere in Rome *wishin'* he was dead! Perhaps in jail. It's a shame, though. Real nice fellow he was."

With a courteous thank you, Onesimus left the fisherman to his mending and went in search of a glass of wine and a little something to eat.

When he finally found a place to his liking he wasn't surprised to find several of the sailors from the Swan and other ships there as well. Sailors and other travelers alike were seated in the sunny courtyard of a small tavern not too far from the docks and they were all eating and talking together like old friends. He joined the small talk about destinations and length of time at sea (each sailor trying to outdo the last) until he finally heard someone mention Adramyttium and the ship the region had lost in a storm the previous fall.

"Aye! 'Twas a loss for certain!" the traveler said. "I'm from Adramyttium myself and I know the owner of the ship. 'Twas one of only three ships he runs. The cargo alone was worth the cost of another ship . . . hauling barley!" The man shook his totally bald head and muttered as if to himself, "No! I'll never be able to understand it! The gods certainly have a peculiar way of dealing with those who obey them!"

The speaker watched the red-faced and perspiring landlord hustling his serving wenches back and forth with plates heaped high with lamb-stuffed grape leaves, crispy-crusted bread fresh from the oven, and bottles of wine, and he shook his head.

"Me! I've never held much with sacrificing. And I've never had much bad luck, either!" he continued.

Onesimus spoke up, "Was that the ship that had the prisoners on their way to trial before Caesar?"

"Aye!" the man nodded so vigorously it seemed he'd probably made himself bald by shaking all the hair out of his scalp. "But there was a prisoner aboard who saved everyone's lives when he warned the sailors not to take to the lifeboat. Then, when the guards wanted to kill the prisoners to keep them from escaping, their commander told them no. All were saved by swimming or floating to shore on the wreckage after the ship ran aground and broke up."

"Was this the same man who..." Onesimus began but the speaker cut him short.

"Oh aye! The very same. 'Twas the same night they straggled ashore. All wet and shivering cold they were so this man, this prisoner... Petros? No... Paulus, I believe, started a fire to warm them and was tending it. He started to gather heavier wood to feed it, but when he tossed an armful of dry wood onto the fire the crew all heard him give a shout of surprise. When they rushed over to him there was a viper that was almost a meter long hanging from his hand!"

The man paused to take a bite of his dinner and continued, "Well, sir! I know you'll never believe me but the owner of the ship was aboard and he, *himself,* will testify that that man walked over as calmly as if he were putting a pot of water to boil in his own home and just easy-like shook that snake off into the fire as if it were nothing! Everyone from the wreck was convinced he must be a murderer or some other evil person the gods wouldn't permit to escape his judgment.

"By Neptune's beard! Those seamen, and prisoners, and guards, the whole lot of 'em, all stood around watching this Paulus as he went about gathering more wood and making sure that everyone had a place near the fire. They expected him, you see, to blow up like a pig's bladder and die right there on the spot . . . but he never did!

"Of course, word traveled like Jupiter's thunderbolts, and it wasn't long before the people of Malta started bringing flowers and fruit and other offerings to lay at his feet, because they believed he must be a god to be able to survive the bite of a viper."

The raconteur's eyebrows knit together as he shook his head in puzzlement, "But he refused to be worshiped! He insisted he was just a man and told them he would accept some of their gifts as gifts for the shipwrecked crew and prisoners but he insisted that they were not to treat him as a god!"

The man, having told the whole story with only a single bite, suddenly remembered his food. He bent over his plate and began shoveling it into his mouth with a will. Then, looking up at Onesimus he said with his mouth full, "That's it. 'Twas a viper; the prisoner insisted he was not a god; no more can be said!"

Onesimus cocked his head to one side as he watched the man consume much of his repast in a seemingly single-minded manner that reminded him of many of his accounting tutors at their books.

"Indeed!" he murmured, "What more *can* be said?"

CHAPTER THIRTEEN

Even though Onesimus enjoyed his three days in Syracuse, spending his time talking to the citizens and taking walks in the countryside and along the shoreline, he was glad once again to be leaning on the deck railing finally and watching the island slip below the horizon.

One more voyage and he would be ready to travel overland to Rome where he felt surely that he could get lost among the crowds, never to be found.

On the second day, as he was trying his hand at climbing the mast, Captain Alban came by and motioned him down.

"It's mighty brave you are!" the captain began with a grin. "Not many landlubbers be for climbing the mast."

Onesimus just shrugged. "Better to risk a broken neck than to never risk anything and die wondering what you *might* have done."

Alban's eyes narrowed and he measured Onesimus once again.

"Well, boy . . . I've got some'at on my mind and I've decided to get rid of it by giving it to you," he said.

At Onesimus' nod Alban said, "I've seen you learning to splice lines and climb the mast... I've watched you work with a will to remove a danger while others might have stayed in their beds and refused to do anything to help. I know you became mighty ill during the blow, but believe it or not so did I on my first voyage and there wasn't a blow of any kind, big or little!

"I've learned that you're a good man and a hard worker and I'd like to offer you a place on my crew!"

Onesimus lost the ability to breathe and with it the ability to speak for a second as he considered what Alban had said. What an opportunity! To begin a life that he, himself, decided upon and not the life his father had planned out for him!

"Captain Alban," he finally began. "I have thought about going to sea and it truly does appeal to me. But..."

Alban interrupted, "I know you've business in Rome. But you could take care of that business and return to Puteoli. This isn't the last time we will dock there and the next time we moor look for me and I'll give you a place on my crew.

Don't make a quick decision, son. Just think about it and if you're interested be certain to be in Puteoli when we return this summer." He thumped Onesimus on the back and walked away, leaving the runaway slave to consider his offer.

Onesimus could barely think of anything else the next few days. He had no trade but bookkeeper and he had no home at all. What a great way to spend the rest of his life! Sailing the Great Sea, seeing the sights, even that great city Alexandria... in fact, seeing all there was to see of the world!

Finally, he approached the captain as he was watching off the starboard side of the ship where dolphins swam along beside the ship, chattering and leaping, as graceful as a frightened deer, but they were not frightened at all.

"Captain Alban, I believe I might take you up on your offer," he began. "But I think I need to tell you the only work I've ever done has been to keep a businessman's accounts. I am trained at that work, but not at physical labor. Not that I'm unwilling to learn but you must know exactly what you're taking on when you take me on to your crew."

Alban smiled, "When you came aboard I saw that your hands were soft and uncalloused. I knew that you were no laborer... but if what you say is true, I could probably use you in your own field! I could use some trained help to get and keep my books straight.

"No matter," he continued. "You have business and so do I. So just think about it and know that the job is open the next time we port in Puteoli!"

"I surely will, Captain."

During the rest of the voyage, Onesimus, true to his word, thought about little else than signing on with the Swan. Perhaps even when the ship reached port, he might sign up. After all, he really had no business in Rome, and he could leave the ship when it docked and then return the next day saying he had been met by a messenger saying his business had been cancelled and he would sign on immediately if the Captain agreed.

As the ship was making the harbor at Puteoli, he decided he would do just that. He would simply disappear for the day and then return the next day acting as if he'd been met by a messenger. He could do it. And why shouldn't he? He'd had his fill of sitting and working at books! He wanted adventure! He wanted the romance of the sea! He wanted to see Alexandria!

So, as he had planned, the minute he was able to go ashore he said good-bye and thank you to the Captain and crew and wandered off down the road toward the center of town. Spending the night wrapped in his cloak in a field beside the road, he found that he could no more sleep now than he had been able to whilst considering the offer. He rolled from side to side and shifted his position and yet couldn't find a spot without a rock under his ribs or a stick poking him in the part of his body that would coincide with the heel of Italy.

At sunup he abandoned the idea of sleeping and rose to wander into town. There, for a few denarii, he was able to purchase some bread and some smoked mussels for a morning feast.

With his hunger abated, he wandered around the town a little more. His plan was to wait until what he felt was an appropriate amount of time before returning to the Swan. He'd been walking the streets for a while when he heard a shout from behind him.

"Boy! Boy!" It was the captain moving toward him at a considerable clip. "I thought you'd be halfway to Rome by now! And, say! You never told me your name!"

Onesimus began to reply with the story he'd concocted when the generous followers of The Way had asked him the same question but the Captain rushed on.

"We're only going to be here about a week, then we're headed back to the eastern regions with a short stop in Ephesus before moving on to Tyre! If you're to sign on with me in the future I need to know who ye be! So ... what is your name?"

Ephesus? Tyre? In a single second all of Onesimus' plans fell away to dust.

Of course he couldn't attach himself to a seafaring bunch! What*ever* had made him think that an oceangoing vessel would never return to the area he had worked so hard and betrayed so many to leave? The story died on his lips and he replied only, "Zacheus. My name is Zacheus and I just needed to stay here overnight so I could find a group of travelers I might attach myself to. I hear it isn't safe to travel alone."

"So it isn't," Alban replied. "I wish you well and I hope to meet with you when we are back in Puteoli this summer. Fare you well, Zacheus!"

Onesimus touched his left shoulder with his right hand in an abbreviated soldier's salute and, muttering a quick good-bye he started back toward the market place where he hoped to find a group of fellow-travelers, as Captain Alban watched him go.

CHAPTER FOURTEEN

Looking back on his life later, Onesimus could see exactly when and where God began stirring into his affairs. All the way from the day of his sale to the slaver there were God's footprints on the pathways of his life.

In his advancing years, he would look upon that day with gratitude and comfort. Yet, the first time God's presence became eminently clear to him was still in the future as he walked into the Puteoli marketplace.

It was moving toward dusk when he learned that there was only one caravan heading toward Rome at this time and it carried prisoners bound for trial before Caesar. While a more timid soul might have quailed at traveling in close quarters with thieves and murderers, that was nothing to him. He was anxious enough to get lost in the crowds of the city that he didn't hesitate to approach the caravan master about joining up with him.

"I suppose the gods are with you," the caravan master, a Centurion, said. "We were supposed to be in Rome four months ago, but one thing after another has kept us from reaching our destination!" The master shook his head remembering his past trials, but he was amenable, so

Onesimus rolled up in his cloak with the rest of the caravan to await first light when they would begin their nine-day trek toward their release or their doom. As Onesimus thought of that phrase he realized that he, too was headed toward release or doom in his own way. That thought brought a weight of discomfort he wasn't happy to welcome.

The clink of the prisoner's chains and shouts of the guards awakened him the following morning.

Hastily he tore a piece of bread from one of the loaves he had bought the day before, thankful that he'd had the forethought to buy a few simple provisions for his journey.

It wasn't until after he had prepared to leave that Onesimus became aware of another man, not a soldier, who was talking with the Captain of the Guard. The man was small and wiry, with a fringe of pepper and salt hair that stood out all around his head, eyes that bulged and a nose like a hawk's beak. Onesimus watched him as he held up his wrists and made a slashing movement across his left wrist. The Captain listened intently and then followed the man to one of the prisoners who was standing under a sycamore tree.

As the two approached, the prisoner held out his chained wrists. Even Onesimus, standing several meters away, could see the suppurating sores where the iron bands had worn away the skin and maybe even some of the muscle in the man's left wrist. The captain crossed again toward one of the pack mules kneeling on the ground and pulled out two skins and some rags. He walked back toward the prisoner and opened the first skin. From it, he poured a little wine into the wounds. From the second bag, he poured some oil onto some rags and then tucked the rags between the iron band and the man's wrist.

While this was taking place Onesimus was slowly moving toward the two men, and soon was close enough to hear the captain talking in a low voice to the wiry man.

"Have you prayed for him yet?"

The wiry man grinned and blinked his eyes slowly. "Not yet. I was led to show you what Cyril is suffering first. Now I shall pray for him!"

The captain shook his head slowly, stepped back a pace and crossed his arms as if he already knew what was coming.

The petitioner first asked a couple of questions of Cyril that Onesimus couldn't hear. Then he placed both hands over the iron wrist band and simply said, "In the name of Jesus Christ . . . be healed!"

Cyril's eyes widened and tears flowed down his cheeks as he shouted, "It's warm! OOHHH! It's so warm!"

After a short span, the captain stepped forward again and gently began removing the cloth from between Cyril's wrist and shackle.

"Go ahead and pull it out captain!" Cyril said. "It doesn't hurt at all!"

Onesimus edged closer as the last rag was removed and the shackle was pushed up Cyril's arm out of the way. There were no sores. There were no scars. There was nothing to show that only minutes ago, Cyril had been facing the loss of his hand, if not his life, from a dangerous infection. Cyril knew it, the Captain of the Guard knew it, the man who prayed knew it, and Onesimus knew it. Yet, of those four, only Onesimus wasn't sure what to make of it.

The guard growled quietly, "Why do you bother calling me over here? You knew you wouldn't need my help after you prayed for him!" Then he turned and walked away. Only Onesimus could see the Centurion's face and notice the secret little smile that played around his lips.

Forgetting himself, and the circumstances, Onesimus walked boldly up to the praying man and spoke quietly, "Who *are* you?"

"I am merely a prisoner of Yeshua the Chosen One and I am His servant. My name is Paulus," he said with a smile.

"Paulus?" asked Onesimus. "The same Paulus who was on the ship out of Adramyttium?"

"The same," Paulus replied.

Onesimus could think of nothing more to say. He just stood there, looking into the gray eyes of this small, sinewy man with the halo of frizzy hair.

"We'll talk more later," Paulus finally said. "Right now it's time to leave and I'm certain you have much to ask me. If you don't mind walking with the prisoners I think we could talk as we journey."

The runaway realized with a start that this man was a prisoner. A man bound for trial before Caesar. Probably a felon . . . so why was he not chained as the others were? Was he a Roman citizen? He pondered whether to ask that particular question, knowing it might be considered rude to call attention to his unfettered state . . . and whom should he ask? He was certain he shouldn't ask the Captain of the Guards. After all, it was possible that Paulus had slipped his chains and the Captain hadn't noticed. He wouldn't want to be responsible for calling attention to the prisoner's inadvertent freedom.

But then, he was afraid that if he asked Paulus himself, the man would get angry with him and refuse to talk at all. It was even possible, after what Onesimus had seen him do, that he might get irate enough to call down fire to devour Onesimus where he stood! As he stood there wondering, a smile moved across Paulus' face as if he knew what Onesimus had been thinking. Even though he thought Paulus perfectly capable of calling down fire if he wanted to, Onesimus decided to walk beside this insignificant-looking little man in hopes of gleaning more information about the viper rumor.

The journey began with the guards' impatient "Come on, come on!" The clanking of prisoners' chains, the shuffling of dusty feet, the braying of the pack mules, and the nickering and huffing of the Guards' horses made for a noisy beginning as they moved up the hill, following a well-trodden path toward the town of Capua and the Appian Way. This road would take them to their final destination.

After they had gone about a half-league Paulus spoke.

"You're wondering why I am allowed to move about freely and wear no chains," he began. "I started out as all the others. I was chained while in bonds in Caesarea, but when the officials realized I was a Roman citizen they removed the chains. Apart from that, the guards pay me little mind because several things have happened along the way that made it clear to my keepers that I wasn't going to try to escape. They decided to allow me the freedom of movement I now enjoy."

Onesimus didn't say anything but nodded his head to indicate his understanding.

Paulus continued, "You're also wondering if the rumors about the viper are true. They are. That is, unless they've given me the status of a god again! I am only a man. But the God I serve protected me from the bite of the viper just as He will protect me from anyone or anything that would do me harm.

That doesn't mean I cannot die . . . on the contrary, I will die whenever God decides the time is right. That could be today or it could be in a hundred years! I am content to let Him decide. For those who are called to serve Him there can be only peace knowing that no matter what happens in our lives, He will turn everything to our good! You've heard of this God before, I know. The Spirit of God spoke to me in the night and has told me much about you . . .," he leaned in close and whispered, "Useful One!"

"You know running away never solved anything," he concluded.

At that simple statement, Onesimus felt his knees go weak. He had heard people say their heart stopped for a moment at the discovery of a shocking revelation, but had always thought they were just exaggerating. But now, he *knew* his own heart had stopped. He felt it stutter in his chest. He was frightened. He felt he should beg this man to say nothing but couldn't get his mouth to work. He could feel his hands trembling... and even his lips were shaking. Fear had grasped hold of him and was not about to let go. If Paulus should inform the guards that he was a runaway slave, his life wouldn't be worth a single copper!

After what seemed an eternity Paulus looked at him and smiled. "I won't reveal your secret until you tell me I can."

Onesimus closed his eyes and gave a sigh. He knew that many men might say they wouldn't tell and then would turn around and betray that promise. But he knew also, deep within his being, that Paulus meant what he'd said. He had no intention of betraying the fugitive slave. And Onesimus had no intention of *ever* telling him he could reveal his terrible secret.

Paulus then swerved into another subject. He spoke quietly. "Within the last year you have experienced great loss and immense sorrow. You have felt great anger and pain. But now you know the truth. You have already seen the reality of the God I serve. You have heard the name Yeshua and you have seen great things done in his name. You know He is the God of gods. Yet, you are still running from Him as surely as you are running from your master. And as I said before, running away is not the answer you seek.

Paulus looked deep into Onesimus' eyes and the fugitive felt his heart begin beating again ... a slow, heavy beat that made him feel as if Paulus could see inside his very soul. It beat so hard that it made his chest hurt.

"You have been thinking about this for a long time. You've been thinking about what you needed to do all the time you dwelt with the widow woman and repaired her home. I even know *how* you would think about it. Your heart would remind you of all you had learned and then you would make yourself busy doing something so you couldn't think about it anymore. You saw believers in the marketplace and knew them for who they were ... sometimes you even longed to become a part of them because you missed the wonderfully mysterious psalms, and hymns, and sermons, and prophecies you witnessed in your master's gatherings. Sometimes, you even tried to find where the local body of believers was meeting so you could join them.

"You know what I mean when I say the time is now for you to make a final decision. You know that Yeshua is the true God and that following Him is the only way you can ever find peace. Your decision must come soon Useful One, because if you delay too long you will never find your way."

Onesimus closed his eyes for a second and nodded.

"I know," he replied seriously. "You have spoken words of truth to me and I know that you are right. It is only because I know that Rome is becoming more and more hostile toward your sect and I fear that hostility will grow into hatred and outright persecution. I dread to think of the fate you and many of your fellow-believers may have to face. I'm..."

"You're afraid," Paulus said gently. "It is a frightening thing to know you have become the enemy of the most powerful government in the world. That you might die just because you believe in something the government fights. When you know that there is a life beyond this life though, and that we all must stand before the God of Creation sooner or later, it changes things. Then you should realize that THAT should be even more frightening to you since His judgment is eternal!"

Paulus reached out his hand and patted Onesimus on the arm. "Be sure . . . but be sure you don't wait too long!"

Without even thinking about it, Onesimus nodded his head. He would be sure. . . . he was pretty close already.

CHAPTER FIFTEEN

The days that followed were filled with Onesimus walking and talking with Paulus as the soldiers shouted at the prisoners to move faster. The prisoners' chains clinked and rattled a rhythm that became almost hypnotic in its regularity. The snap of the whip was a sound heard often as one of the soldiers tired of issuing verbal rebukes to a dawdling captive. These prisoners, with the exception of Paulus, were not known to be citizens of Rome. They were citizens of nations currently subjugated to Rome.

The nights were filled with tossing and turning, chasing and trying to catch the elusive and much desired goal of sleep while thoughts of Yeshua and His followers pursued Onesimus round and round as he lay wrapped in his cloak. Onesimus knew the truth of Philemon's God but continued to hesitate to embrace him. He also knew as well as anyone what fate might very well await those who were discovered to be followers of this different God; a god who demanded the single-minded loyalty of his subjects. Caesar was growing more and more tired of this new religion who denied the gods of Rome and Greece and even the deity of Caesar, himself! How long would it be before outright oppression and harassment would be the common lot of these uncommon folk?

Even when he did manage to fall asleep, it did him no good. *In his dream-filled sleep he saw himself standing in the garden of his home. The scent of hibiscus fills the air and his ears are filled with the sound of the water fountain in the center of the garden. His mother enters by the gate from the narrow pathway behind the house. Her still-black, waist-length hair gleams in the early twilight. She looks at him, startled and then frowns. "Who are you?" She demands angrily. "What do you want here?"*

"Mother! It's me. Onesimus!"

She shakes her head. "Onesimus? I've never heard of Onesimus! Why are you here bothering our family?!?"

He falls on his knees before her. "Mother! Mother! I am your second son! You MUST know me! You MUST!"

He jerked himself upright and awake and was dismayed to realize his cheeks were wet. He swiped at the tears and lay back to sleep, and soon began to dream again.

This time Onesimus found himself back at Philemon's house and he is listening to someone tell their dream during the meeting.

"I saw a great beast whose claws and teeth ripped and tore at the body of Christ. Destruction was upon every person who proclaimed the Name!" The speaker looks directly at Onesimus and cries, "But this destruction was nothing

compared to the terrors awaiting those who knew the truth but refused to bow their knee!"

Philemon looks over at him and shakes his head in sorrow. "So sad! So sad," he moans. "I would have had a new brother if you had only yielded to his calling! As it is, your fate is sealed; your time is almost up! Turn now for you will not have another chance!"

The Governor who attends grabs him by the arm and begins to shake him. The shaking goes on for a long time until, finally . . .

Onesimus jerked awake with a hand on his arm, shaking him.

"Friend! You must have had a terrible dream!" Paulus exclaims in a low voice. "You were moaning and thrashing around. It's a wonder the guards didn't awaken."

The runaway shook his head and rubbed his face vigorously with his hands. "Oh, Paulus! Thank you for waking me. It was indeed a frightful dream!"

"Well, if you can try to get a little more sleep," Paulus said tenderly. "We've several days ahead of us on this road and you need to start each day fresh if you can."

Onesimus nodded and begged Paulus, "Pray that my sleep will be quiet?" Paulus smiled and nodded as the runaway, trusting that this time there would be no more dreams, lay down again.

The next day was "more of the same." An apple for breakfast and the dullness of placing one foot in front of the other time after time after time until time and most everything else was forgotten in a fog of boredom.

It was mid-morning before Onesimus asked Paulus the one question he had yet to answer.

"How did you come to believe in this Chosen One?"

"It is an amazing story, my friend. I had just finished seeing to the 'disciplining' of several Jews who had begun to teach that Yeshua was the Messiah. I had been amazed at the peace these Jews displayed in the face of severe punishment. In fact, it hadn't been long since I had assisted in the stoning of a man named Stephen. When he was first taken, he preached a grand teaching about the Messiah and proved to all present that Yeshua must be that man but when he cried out, 'Behold, I see the heavens opened, and the Son of man standing on the right hand of God' it made us angry and we mobbed him and dragged him to the place of stoning where we killed him. I, being a righteous Pharisee, did not participate, but held the cloaks of those who did. Before he died, I heard Stephen pray for all of us who were involved. As the stones began to strike him he looked at me and cried out loudly, 'Father, do not charge them with this crime.' Then he died.

"After that first stoning, I was charged by the Sanhedrin with doing all I could to put down this movement. So, traveling all over the region, I spent my days hunting down 'heretical' Jews.

"Well, the day of my conversion, I was going to bring a group of these believers from Damascus back to Jerusalem to be punished.

"As I neared Damascus about noon, suddenly there shone from heaven a great light all around me. It was so brilliant it startled me and I fell to the ground covering my face. Then I heard a voice saying to me, 'Saul, Saul, why do you persecute me?'

"Without thinking, I asked, 'Who are you, Lord?' The reply came back as clear as my speech to you, 'I am Jesus of Nazareth, whom you are persecuting.'

"They that were with me saw the light, and were afraid; but they didn't hear the voice that spoke to me. And I said, 'What shall I do, LORD?' And the voice said, 'Get up. Go into Damascus and there you will hear all things which are planned for you to do.'

"It was then that I realized that I couldn't see. Not because the light had been so bright, but because God wanted me to sit still and listen for a while, so I was led by the hand into Damascus by those who accompanied me. It was a fearful time! Would I ever see again? Had Jesus of Nazareth gotten so angry with me that I would be reduced to begging for my food? It was a good thing that my traveling companions were people I had known a long time because they could have led me into the surrounding countryside and beaten and robbed me of all I had and I would have been helpless before them.

"Once we reached Damascus I stayed with a friend for three days and neither ate nor drank during that time. It was there I met Ananias, a devout man who followed the law of Moses. He had a good reputation among all the Jews who lived there.

"He came to me and said, 'Brother Saul, receive thy sight.' Something like scales fell from my eyes and right then I was able to see again.

"He went on, saying, 'The God of our fathers has chosen you to know his will. He allowed you to hear his voice because you will be his witness to the Gentiles and also to the Jews about what you have seen and heard.'

"As I told you, I had spent three days fasting. Along with that I had prayed steadily to understand what was happening and what would happen to me.

"As soon as Ananias came in and laid his hands upon me, I entered the waters of baptism and arose a new man in Christ Jesus."

Paulus stopped speaking and wisely allowed all the details of the story to sink deep into the mind and heart of his hearer.

Onesimus, too, walked in silence contemplating all he had been told. He was having trouble imagining this mild man taking part in stonings and other terrible punishments. It was far beyond his ability to comprehend.

They had traveled probably a league or more before he spoke again.

"So you went ahead and were baptized and then began teaching about this new Way?"

"Yes. As I said, I *was* baptized. And I did preach the Anointed One in the synagogues, but I had to calm the fears of those believers who had also been following Yeshua. Many of them thought my conversion was a trick and it took a bit to persuade them that I really HAD decided to become one of them."

"Do you think 'decided' is the right word?" Onesimus responded. "It sounds almost as if you were without a say in this decision!"

Paul laughed. "Not at all. When Ananias said, 'God has chosen you,' he only meant that God knew from the very beginning of time that I would choose to follow Him wherever He led me so He had a whole plan for my life!

"I could have chosen to NOT follow God's leading. We all have that ability. But God knew from before time began that when I was given a clear choice I would choose to go His way."

The conversation kept going until the break at noon and through the meal, meager though it was, and on into the afternoon of walking. To be sure, there were silences as well as talk, but Onesimus tried to keep them to a minimum to hold back the uneasy thoughts that came with quiet.

With this companionship, the time passed relatively quickly and Onesimus was almost sad to see it end when finally the sun stood close to the western horizon and the soldiers were securing their prisoners for the night.

"And what of you, my dear friend?" Paul continued softly. "Have you thought more about my conversion and about Yeshua and His claims?"

Suddenly Onesimus felt the sting of tears and blinked them away. He had been thinking about it and he knew Paulus and all those he had met at Philemon's home and that couple who lived by the Way ... they were all right. Yeshua was the Son of God and He *was* the God of Creation.

More than that, the words spoken by Paulus about holding nothing but peace and forgiveness for those who wronged him awoke in Onesimus a longing to feel that way about those who had wronged him. He ached to be at peace with his father and brother even though they had cast him aside as one would cast aside a broken stylus. He wanted to feel something besides disappointed puzzlement in his mother's seeming abandonment of his cause.

"Yes!" he whispered softly. "Death and Heaven are better by far than life and bitterness! I believe!"

Paulus smiled through the dark and talked for several more minutes to Onesimus, showing him The Way and welcoming him to the family of God.

And, for the first time in a long time, Onesimus fell asleep and slept soundly without dreams of abandonment and anger.

The next few days were filled with walking and learning about "The Way" as the followers of the Christ called it.

He learned not only some basic Hebrew Scriptures from Isaiah and the Psalms but also the details of the crucifixion and resurrection of Yeshua. Paulus was also careful to describe how members of the Body of Christ could recognize one another and talked to him about the need for caution in the face of growing opposition.

It was on the seventh night that the boredom of the trek was broken.

Once again, the prisoners had been secured, the campfires had almost died and the guards, who had been talking among themselves, had settled down for the night.

Onesimus and Paulus were lying next to each other, wrapped in their cloaks and on the verge of sleep. Paulus raised his head, listening intently.

"What is it?" Onesimus asked in a whisper.

"Shhh," Paulus replied. "I heard the brush rustling. Something or someone is creeping up on the camp."

Just then Onesimus heard it, too.

The guards had often chosen similar places to camp on the trip. It was a cleared place, not too far off the road but far enough to be protected from foot traffic. Some of the guards had argued against stopping here because the cleared place was surrounded on three sides by brush and high grasses. This meant that, in their eyes, there was too much cover to use by those who meant harm to the caravan by stealing food or weapons or even assisting in an escape. Even so, the commander decided it was good enough and ordered the camp to be set up.

Now, Onesimus was beginning to think those who had opposed this site had been right. What was out there? Was it a partner of one of the prisoners trying to come to their rescue? Was it a deer or a sheep just walking through the brush on the way to better pasturage? Onesimus realized his nerves were humming. Slowly he sat up and peered through the darkness toward the encroaching brush.

He heard a hiss of breath from Paulus' lips, "Over there by the guards' area. Look closely," Paulus whispered. "Wolves."

Onesimus peered into the darkness and suddenly, picking up a dim glimmer from the coals of the fires, glowing eyes became visible. There were . . . one, two, three . . . four. Four pairs of shining, golden eyes blinking and slinking closer to the encampment. Without talking about it or even thinking about it, Onesimus and Paulus both simultaneously sat up and shouted.

The camp became a melee of shouts and cursing and the wolves, understandably, melted into the night.

"Here!" the watch was walking toward the two responsible for waking up the whole encampment. "What do you think you're doing screaming out like that!" he said angrily.

Onesimus spoke up. "Wolves. There were wolves coming through the bushes toward the guard's bedding area. Four of them!"

Paulus chimed in, "That's right. They were skulking around and we were afraid they were going to attack, so we cried out to chase them off or to waken you if they were too hungry to be frightened."

"Wolves!" the guard replied. "What nonsense! We're too close to the road to be bothered by wolves. Beyond that, it's summer with plenty of prey for the wolves. What makes it even more impossible is that I've just finished taking a stroll around the perimeter of the camp and I saw nothing! Besides, wolves don't come near humans unless they are starving," he exclaimed. "Who do you think you're dealin' with? Somebody without a brain?"

A call came from across the clearing, "Fulvius! They are right. There *were* wolves!"

The Captain of the Guard had lit a torch from the fading embers and was moving it slowly above the ground. "There were at least four of them and those men probably saved our miserable lives when they shouted like that. Especially yours," he said as he showed the paw prints to the returning guard and anyone else who wished to see. "One of those fellows was very big and probably quite hungry. It looks like they were approaching the place where *you* were sleeping, Fulvius!"

Fulvius took a single look at the prints and then glanced over at the duo who had, in all likelihood, saved his life. He frowned and grumbled and then lifted his left hand and made an odd motion as if he were throwing something toward them as he turned away and picked up his cloak in preparation to lie back down. But he didn't lie down in the same place; instead, he moved toward the center of the clearing where he promptly rolled over and at least pretended to be instantly asleep.

The eighth day passed similarly to the previous seven days without incident except for a short stop when one of the guard's horses stepped in a hole and went down. The guard struggled to act as if it wasn't important to him that his mare might have to be put down. But every man there knew better. This was his horse. His companion through many miles and many dangers and he cared deeply about her. In a short while he was unable to control himself and he wept. Even with tears streaming down his face, he was readying his short sword to do what must be done for a horse with a broken leg when Paulus moved around to kneel beside her. He ran his hands over her head and down her forehead, over her huffing nostrils and her muzzle, talking to her all the time. After soothing the horse, he moved into position at the horse's broken pastern bone and gently placed his hands close to the swelling break. The horse calmed a little more and Paulus closed his eyes and just knelt there. The Captain of the Guard sidled over to Onesimus and muttered, "Humans are one thing, but I can't believe his God is going to care about a dumb animal!"

Onesimus had nothing much to say so he just looked into the captain's eyes until the horse gave a loud snort and began struggling to stand up. A collective gasp from the on-looking guards signaled that something surprising was occurring. Onesimus and the guard turned as a man to see what was happening.

The owner of the horse dropped his sword on the ground, grabbed his mount's reins and did what he could to help his struggling horse to stand. Then he ran his hands down the formerly swollen and obviously broken leg. Shaking his head, his open mouth declaring his shock, he said quietly, "It's not broken. She's fine. She's just fine!" Then, unable to hide his joy, he threw his arms around the neck of his mare and wept aloud.

The captain just shook his head and began to rally the travelers to continue their trek. Onesimus noticed that his hands were trembling.

At the end of that momentous day, the group of guards, prisoners, and Onesimus stood at the top of one of Rome's famous seven hills looking down into the city. It had taken them until late afternoon to reach this place and the Captain of the Guard had called a halt to the caravan until morning. The last of Onesimus' supplies served as his supper, except for one hard biscuit and a small piece of cheese he saved for morning.

For one more night Onesimus wrapped his cloak around himself and prepared for sleep, as he wondered aloud to a nearby Paulus how quiet the prisoners were this night.

Paulus spoke into the darkness, "It's because they are going to their judgment soon. For many it may mean the end of their life. For others..." Paulus shifted slightly. "...it could mean enslavement or years in the prisons of Rome. That, my friend, is not a pleasant thought unless you're particularly fond of lice, rats, damp, dark and chains!"

"What about you?" Onesimus asked with a slight quiver in his voice. "What sentence do you face?"

The dying coals of the campfires illuminated the ground enough so that he could see Paulus shake his head slightly as he replied, "Because I am a Roman citizen, I will not await trial in jail, but my sentence will be whatever the Lord allows. You know that it is becoming clearer every day that we Christians have no need to be guilty of any crime to be put to death. Whatever my sentence, rest assured that, as I have told you before, I hold only peace and forgiveness for those who will carry it out because if I live, I have more time to work for Yeshua... and if I die I go to live with Him forever."

The fugitive pondered the words of his mentor as he drifted toward sleep. Would he ever be able to say what Paulus had said? He still felt ugly feelings for his father and brother, although the hatred was gone and the bitterness had lessened a great deal. He no longer dreamed dreams of betrayal and he no longer daydreamed of seeing his father and brother in chains of slavery as they had bound him. As he talked to his new Father, he asked Him to continue to wash his heart and mind clean of all bitterness and pain and to give him a new heart of forgiveness. Then he slept.

Onesimus woke on the ninth day knowing that if all went well he would be in Rome by day's end. That thought brought an odd wave of regret with it because their conversations, and Onesimus' conversion, had brought a closeness between Paulus and Onesimus that reminded the truant slave of his previous relationship with his own brother, Protos. He decided to tell that to Paulus once they were on the move again.

After breaking fast, the caravan readied themselves for one more short day of travel. They set out, some hoping to reach Rome quickly and some wishing Rome would somehow disappear before they arrived.

It took them from just after sunrise until midday to move down into the city where the calls of vendors and the laughter of young mothers visiting vied for the listeners' attentions with shouts of "Stop! Thief!" as a young man came from behind and pelted past the travelers.

Just as the boy was about to make his escape good though, Onesimus was amused to see one of the guards casually stretch out his hand and grab the thief by the scruff of the neck and shake him. He didn't even bother to look at the miscreant when he did it. He just continued his conversation with his companion while it seemed his hand decided all on its own to grab the runner and give him a good shaking until the vendor-victim arrived to snatch back the loaf of bread and wedge of cheese the boy was carrying under his arm.

But as amusing and interesting as the sounds and sights of Rome were, the smells were what grabbed the hungry traveler by the nose and dragged him along.

Smells, good and bad, lingered on the air together tempting Onesimus one minute and nauseating him the next.

A spit turned above a fire and the smell of roasting lamb was almost more than Onesimus could bear as he thought of all those nights with nothing but stale bread and sour wine to eat and drink! But he needn't have worried long about the temptation because next door to the wonderful aroma, a woman was emptying her slops into the street. Just beyond that a baker was thrusting a long wooden paddle into an oven to remove fresh bread that was almost aromatic enough to make Onesimus forget the other smells.

Paulus managed to work his way to Onesimus' side. "Come with us as far as the prison gate," he said. "I have several things to tell you before I leave you."

At Onesimus's nod, Paulus began, "First, while I am a Roman citizen and cannot be held in prison, I will probably be held under house arrest. That means I'm going to need a house! So, when you leave me travel two streets to the west and you will find a large limestone building on the corner. The door has a fish carved into it. Knock on the door and when they answer, tell them Paulus sends you. After you're inside tell them your story . . . you can trust them . . . and they will help you learn what you must know and you will be able to let them know I have arrived. That part is important because I need to find some sort of accommodations quickly and I depend upon these fellow Christians to help me with that."

Onesimus took careful note of the streets and byways as they passed toward the jail where Paulus would spend a short time and those not lucky enough to be Roman citizens would be kept until their trials.

Even though Onesimus was aware that he and Paulus had become fast friends, he was surprised at the depth of feeling he experienced when it came time to part. It was as if he were leaving his father at the prison gate.

After Paulus had been taken away Onesimus steeled himself and called to mind the directions Paulus had given him. He easily found the large limestone house with the fish carved in the door. He knocked on the door and waited until the door opened. Two young men, identical in appearance, stood before him as he uttered the words Paulus had told him to say.

They led him into the house and ran to find their parents, leaving him standing in the hallway.

CHAPTER SIXTEEN

I left him at the gates of the prison just before I came here," Onesimus concluded his tale in the presence of a household of believers.

They had ushered him directly into the salon and offered him figs and grapes and good wine as they asked him about Paulus and how he had fared on the journey.

"Well, even though he will be free shortly, I've no doubt he would like some sort of food," Agapetus, the father of the family said. "I'm going to go see when he will be ready to leave that place. Prepare a small basket of food, Perpetua. I'll take it with me."

Perpetua, the family cook, hurried toward the kitchen to prepare a quick repast the Master could take with him.

The Mistress of the home spoke quietly, "Husband, perhaps I should attend you? I would like to meet our dear brother."

"That wouldn't be wise, Agnes dearest. There will be time over the next few days and weeks when you will be able to talk with him, I'm sure. Right now, I would like to make certain that those guarding him are, if not kindly-natured, at least not inclined to hold him any longer than necessary."

His wife nodded, "Perhaps you're right."

Onesimus watched this exchange in surprise. His own mother would have insisted on going and a long and loud argument would have followed. This way of relating husband to wife was so far away from what he had known as a child he could only marvel at the loving exchange and quick acquiescence of Agnes. There was no sign of threat from Agapetus and no sign of fear from Agnes. It was just taken as proper that Agapetus had the final say.

Matthias, Agapetus' footman, assisted his Master with his cloak and took the basket from the capable hands of Perpetua. He then held the open door for his Master and stepped onto the street to attend him in his errand. Agapetus lay his hand on his manservant's arm, "You needn't go if you don't wish to," he said gently.

Matthias smiled and replied, "Sir! I wouldn't miss this opportunity for all the Centurions in Rome."

Agapetus said nothing, he just chuckled and nodded.

When the door was closed the women excused themselves to tend to household duties. Before she left, Agnes informed Onesimus that he was more than welcome to lie down on one of the couches and rest until Agapetus returned.

After that, there were left in the salon just the two young men who had allowed him into the house. There were about thirteen and no matter how he tried, Onesimus could not see a freckle of difference between them. He was a little bemused by them because they were mirror images of each other. Thomas and Timothy were twins.

They seemed to be utterly taken by this stranger who had entered their home with no warning. They had heard his tale of prisoners and healings and a holy man they had heard stories about for as long as they could remember. A man who wrote letters that guided their family's whole life. For a short span, Onesimus and the two boys just sat and stared at each other. Then the twins looked at each other for a minute and began to speak.

Thomas began, "What's your name? You never told us your name."

Onesimus' heart began to pound and he began to pull out the story he had adopted as his own. He opened his mouth to say, "Zacheus" but, instead he said, "My name is Onesimus. My father sold me into slavery to pay his debts and I ran away from my Master before I believed. Now, I am hoping that other Christians can help me make amends for all the wrong things I am guilty of."

Timothy and Thomas looked at each other again and this time Timothy spoke, "We're too young to help much but I'm sure father and Paulus together can help you."

Thomas took up the conversation, "And you don't need to worry. We won't tell anyone anything. We're very good at keeping secrets."

Onesimus smiled and nodded, "I am certain you are. My brother and I were when I was your age!" His use of that phrase seemed to strike him in the heart and, for the first time, he realized he was no longer a "young man." Between his experiences, his newfound faith and his years he had become a man.

CHAPTER SEVENTEEN

fter the boys had silently consulted each other they left the room so quietly and slowly they seemed to dissipate in the air like the steam from a boiling pot.

Onesimus took this chance to rest with gratitude and stretched out on one of the salon's couches. His head had no sooner gotten level with his body than he was emitting a sonorous rumble which caused both Agnes and Perpetua to giggle a little when they wandered through the room a little later.

Onesimus had no idea how long he slept that afternoon except that the sun was approaching the horizon when he finally was awakened to the crash of the front door. Raucous laughter echoed through the house and a male voice shouted, "Agnes! Agnes! You wished to meet our brother Paulus in person and now you may! He will be spending a time with us until he finds accommodations."

Sleep muzzy, Onesimus remained horizontal where he was until that familiar piece of human wire stood over him, arms akimbo. "Well! Amazing how much you can sleep, boy! Did you have trouble sleeping on your feather bed last night?"

Agnes came down the stairs quickly and entered the salon just as Onesimus came upright. Perpetua and the twins followed close behind her as she almost jogged up to her new guest.

"Dear, this is our brother Paulus who has guided us into our new life without ever having met us," Agapetus said. "Boys, be polite and greet our guest! Paulus, this is Thomas and Timothy our sons and that quiet creature over there . . ." this spoken wryly since the object of his attention was nearly bouncing up and down in her eagerness to meet Paulus for herself, "is our cook, Perpetua."

Both boys greeted the newcomer with politeness and Perpetua took his hand and bowed before him.

"Do not do it," Paulus said quietly as he helped her up. "We bow before our Lord, Perpetua. We needn't bow to each other." Paulus then smiled and continued, "However, if that wonderful repast you sent to me is a sample of your cooking, I ought to be bowing before you!"

Perpetua, who seemed to have lost her ability to speak, just blushed and nodded and giggled. She scurried away to the kitchen while Paulus called out to her, "Don't plan for me at supper tonight. I couldn't eat again today after that wonderful feast you sent!"

"Paulus, no doubt you've made yourself a lifelong champion with that exchange. I believe that now, she would take your place before Caesar if she could!" Agapetus said.

"Well, I wouldn't ask it of her, but if she really wants to . . ." Paulus replied with good humor.

Agapetus took him by the arm and led him toward the stairs. "We have a bed prepared for you and I'm certain that if I leave you near it, you will soon be as deeply asleep as our friend was when we came in."

Paulus stopped and looked from Agapetus to Onesimus and back again. "Have you told him anything?" Paulus asked as his eyes met Onesimus'.

"There really wasn't time before he left. I told the boys when they asked my name."

Paulus took Onesimus by one arm and Agapetus by the other and said, "We need to take a walk before I take my leave of you, Agapetus. Let us walk in the garden and talk amongst ourselves."

Agapetus' garden consisted of two parts. The part nearest the kitchen wing of the house was given over to vegetables and herbs for cooking. But unlike many Roman homes, there was room enough to include a second section that was given over to trees, flowers and fountains. It was here the men walked.

Three cypress trees whispered overhead as the three men walked the pathways of the garden and quietly discussed the circumstances of Onesimus' arrival in Rome. The scent of roses filled the air and violets and cyclamen covered the ground. As he was speaking, Onesimus glanced overhead and stopped still. His eyes grew round and his face paled.

"What is it?" Paulus asked with concern.

"Look! An owl! I don't think I want to continue this discussion, Paulus. Please!"

"An owl?!?" Paulus echoed. "Do you yet believe in omens?"

Onesimus closed his eyes. "My last day as my father's son ... just before he told me what was to happen ... I saw an owl gliding overhead. My father always said to see an owl was the worst kind of omen."

"Onesimus! Did not our God make the owls? Did he not create the fish and the birds and everything else and pronounce it good? Owls aren't omens; they are part of God's creation!"

Onesimus opened his eyes. They were dancing with light and his face split open in a wide smile. He again began walking. "You are right. Omens belong to the old gods of Rome. They are nothing to those of us who have bowed before the God of creation." He looked over at Agapetus and then down at the ground as he recounted his flight from Philemon and his fascination with the rumors of a man who seemed immortal.

The excitement of his first encounter with Paulus and when he surrendered to the God of Israel became apparent in his voice and bearing. And, thus, he came to his arrival at Agapetus' doorstep.

Agapetus nodded quietly throughout the tale, looking over at Paulus once in a while until Onesimus wound up his account by saying, "And now I am at your mercy."

"No, no!" Agapetus replied. "You are not at *my* mercy! As my brother in Christ you are at God's mercy alone! And you must realize that if I read the signs aright. It won't be long and everyone who claims the Name of Christ will be outlaws! I could not bar you from my home unless I am willing to do the same to myself and my very own dear family in the near future!"

Paulus chimed in, "I thought I might ask you to assist me in finding a house and when that is accomplished, Onesimus could come stay with me and learn more about The Anointed One and the Way before we make any final moves. He could be a big help to me while he studies."

Agapetus nodded and sucked his teeth a little bit as he thought this through.

"Sounds like a good idea! We can certainly make room for one more until you are settled. In fact, it might be a good idea to allow him to stay in your room while we look—that way his education can begin immediately."

Onesimus stood there, looking from one to the other as the next phase of his future was decided. When Paulus nodded his agreement, Onesimus' heart leapt as he realized he was not to be sent away. He was not to be taken back in chains. He was to stay with his beloved father/brother Paulus for a while longer as he learned the ins and outs of this Gospel he had embraced.

CHAPTER EIGHTEEN

"Onesimus, could you get me a new quill, please?" Paulus called. "This one has died the death and cannot be revived."

Paulus and Agapetus' son, Timothy, had been laboring over this letter throughout the morning. Timothy would write and Paulus would correct. Paulus would write and Timothy would shake his head and correct. Back and forth it had gone all day and Onesimus was just a little put out. After all, *he . . . Onesimus,* was Paulus' official assistant. Why had Paulus felt the need to call in this . . . this *outsider* to do what he had done for Paulus for the last sixteen months? Onesimus hated to admit it, but he was jealous.

Onesimus pulled a new feather from its box and set about creating a quill with his well-honed knife. He set the blade's edge about a finger's width from the end of the quill and pulled gently toward himself. When the curl of feather shaft dropped away, he placed the edge of the knife on the very end of the quill and carefully split the shaft upward about half the length of the previous cut. With the shaping of the quill completed he handed it over to the man he served with joy. He wished for nothing more than to continue this service for as long as he could see into the future.

Since moving into this little house to await trial, Paulus had taught Onesimus everything he could about the Christian faith and, in return, Onesimus had served as eyes and ears in the community for the aging apostle. Only one guard stood duty at the door of the house and most of those who served regularly had become friends if not believers since beginning their duty here.

Although Onesimus wished to remain here serving the man who had shown him the way to eternal life, he knew that sooner or later this idyllic time of his life would come to an end and sooner or later he would have to return to Philemon. He had already told Paulus that he felt he had to do this and Paulus agreed. But Paulus also made it clear that he wouldn't want that to happen until Paulus deemed him well-founded in the faith.

"Paulus, if you won't need me here for a little while, I'd like to go to the marketplace and bring back something for dinner," Onesimus said. "All we have in the house is a little cheese."

Paulus turned from his writing with a furrowed brow.

He looks so sad! Onesimus thought. What could have brought such a sorrowful countenance to this Apostle of Joy?

"Of course, but first I need you to read this for me," Paulus replied. Timothy had taken his leave and mimicking the behavior of Protus on that fateful night, had not looked at Onesimus once. Paulus knew that his handwriting was large and difficult to read for some. He usually allowed Onesimus to write the missive out and then had him read it aloud so that he could add or subtract anything he didn't like. He would sometimes add something in his own handwriting to emphasize a certain thought.

Onesimus stepped over to the desk and pulled up his stool. Paulus reached over and patted his arm.

"It is time, Useful One! You must return to your master and render him service and obedience," he said gently.

Onesimus' heart dropped into his feet. He had known this day was coming. He had thought about the final reckoning daily but had hoped that it could be put off for a long time. He had no idea what Philemon's reaction would be when he stood on the doorstep with this communiqué from Paulus. He was still subject to whatever punishment Philemon regarded as appropriate, and for that reason alone he trembled as he pulled the missive to himself, nervously cleared his throat and began to read aloud.

"*This letter is from Paulus, in prison for preaching the Good News about Christ Jesus, and from our brother Timothy. It is written to Philemon, our much loved co-worker, and to our sister Apphia and to Archippus, a fellow soldier of the cross. I am also writing to the church that meets in your house.*

"*May God our Father and the Lord Jesus Christ give you grace and peace . . .*"

Onesimus closed his eyes for a moment and asked that Paulus's prayer would apply to him as well.

After he had finished reading, he looked up into Paulus' gray eyes and sighed.

"I shall miss you, my father," he said simply.

Paulus looked away and blinked several times. Even so, his eyes were strangely glassy when he turned again to his beloved spiritual son. His voice hoarse, he said, "And I shall miss you as well. But you have learned well the foundations of our faith and now must make amends for those wrongs you did before you believed. It was with great regret that I composed this letter, but I now believe that Philemon will accept you as his brother. My trial is tomorrow and then we will know my fate as well. After that we will make preparation for you to do what must be done. Agreed?"

Onesimus nodded and murmured his consent.

Onesimus wandered around the little house, picking up and putting down various small items, trying to create the illusion of being busy. This waiting was nerve-wracking. Paulus had wanted him to stay here while he went before Caesar, but he should have insisted on attending his beloved teacher and friend.

Now it was midmorning and he still hadn't heard anything. How frustrating this was! Knowing the Roman courts' reputation didn't help his nerves any. Paulus could be gone from his life completely by now because justice in Rome might not always be fair but it was always swift.

Giving up on his attempt to distract himself, Onesimus moved to the doorway and sat on the doorsill. Resting his arms on his knees, he lowered his head and laid it on his forearms. The guard who stood at the door had gone with Paulus to his trial, of course, so for the first time there was no one there to talk with. He rolled his head to the right and gazed down the road, straining to see the first sign of Paulus coming back. He sat there watching from midmorning 'til midday before he began to sink into a nerve-induced daze. He had just reached the coveted level of a trance-like state when someone began shaking his shoulder.

"Onesimus! Wake up! It's over! Paulus is free! He was released immediately." Marcus, the guard was standing over him. "I only came back here to let you know and to take my leave of you. Paulus decided he wanted to stop at Agapetus' home and let everyone waiting there know before coming back here. I am beside myself with joy I don't mind telling you. Without Paulus I would never have found the truth!

"Brother Onesimus I bid you fare thee well. I have one week to spend with my family and then I join my regiment in the north. Pray for me that my time with my parents and brothers will be fruitful for the Christ."

Onesimus, roused from his daze, nodded his head and rose to give his brother, the guard, a hug. "Thank you for coming to tell me! I have been worried about this trial's outcome and I am relieved it is over. Do you think I have time to get to Agapetus' house before Paulus leaves?"

Marcus pondered for a second and responded. "There are probably many people there and Paulus will feel obligated to speak to everyone. I think there is plenty of time," he laughed.

Onesimus closed the door behind himself and hurried eastward toward the home of Agapetus.

If he had never been to that particular neighborhood before ... if he had never heard of Agapetus ... if he had never become a part of a loving family/community ... he still would have been able to point out Agapetus' home as a place of grand celebration this day.

Laughter, talk and even music wafted on the breeze from the open front door of the house to Onesimus' ears before he came within a block. He could detect the distinctive sounds of the Aulos, Kithara and the brazen pans creating melody that emphasized the joy of the household.

Entering the front door, Onesimus was grabbed by the upper arms and pulled into a giant hug. "Useful One! I am so glad you came! How did you hear we were celebrating here?" Agapetus said as he released him from the crushing embrace.

Onesimus told him that Marcus the guard had said Paulus was here. "How did you get the players here so quickly?" he asked.

Agapetus laughed, "We didn't! We brought them in last night, knowing we would be celebrating today! All but the Aulos player ... she was waiting for Paulus at the court and came back here with him, piping all the way! Why don't you go on in and find your teacher? I believe he is in the garden right now."

Onesimus moved away toward the rear of the house where he could see the musicians gathered in the salon. As he moved beyond them, he saw Paulus seeking a quiet moment in the peaceful gardens of Agapetus.

As he hesitated to go out to him, fearing calling attention to his presence in the garden and creating another mob scene, Paulus turned toward him and smiled, gesturing to him to come out.

Stepping quickly outside he crossed the courtyard, passed under the whispering cypress trees, and joined Paulus at the border between flower garden and kitchen garden. Paulus smiled broadly and put his arm around Onesimus' shoulder. "They believed enough to bring umbrellas to a drought!"

Onesimus just smiled. He was struck dumb with gratitude to God for His protection of his spiritual patron.

CHAPTER NINETEEN

I t is all very well and good to say, "You have to go back and face Philemon." Onesimus brooded on the doorsill the next day. But it costs money to travel that far. Even if I travel overland with a caravan it's going to take food money as well as money to purchase an animal for the trip.

When he arrived in Rome he had had money left over. He had been very frugal with Philemon's money on the voyage but when he had joined the Way, he had turned it all over to Paulus because he knew he could no longer use those ill-gotten gains. Paulus had taken the money and Onesimus had no idea what he had done with it after that. He knew beyond knowing that Paulus had not used it because that would not have been in his nature. However, he might have given it to one of the groups of poor believers he knew of in the city.

All Onesimus knew for certain beyond that was that *he* didn't have it . . . and he hadn't had a chance to raise any money for the trip. He knew that God would provide what was needed . . . he always did. But he was curious to see just how He was going to do it.

"My friend! I looked to where you were sitting and realized with surprise that you have a huge black cloud hovering over you!" Paulus said. "What is on your mind?"

Onesimus had known Paulus to state in words exactly what was on a person's mind many times. For a time, he was afraid that nothing he thought was beyond the Apostle's purview, then Paulus explained that sometimes the Holy Spirit would give him special knowledge as a sign to the unbelievers around him. It wasn't that he could read minds . . . it was that he could hear the Holy Spirit telling him what he needed to know.

"I was wondering," Onesimus replied, "just how the Father is going to supply the wherewithal for my travels back to Colossae. I'm not worried about it because I know that at the right time the money will come. But now that you have released me, I can't help but be anxious to be on my way. Not that I want to leave you because you are truly my father but I know this must be done and I want to do it. It has weighed heavily upon me since my early days as a follower of the Christ. Do you . . ."

Paulus smiled, "I know exactly what you mean. And you are right. God will provide the money for your trip exactly when it is time for you to go."

Speaking this way, Paulus walked across the room and opened a door in a cabinet. From it, he pulled a familiar kidskin bag that uttered a distinctive *chink* as he transferred it to his other hand and held it out to Onesimus.

Color rose in Onesimus' face as he recognized the bag. "I thought you had given this money to the poor or had used it for a good cause!" he exclaimed.

"I did," Paulus replied with a smile. "I held it knowing that someday you would be ready to return and would need assistance to get there. I am sure that Philemon would approve and, as you know from my letter to him, which you are going to deliver, I have promised to pay back everything he requires of you."

Paulus tipped his head to the side as he looked at Onesimus. "After all, that *is* what fathers do for their sons," he concluded quietly. Then, gazing steadily into the eyes of his student and nodding slightly, he once again held out the bag. "Take it and go find a decent mount for the trip overland."

Onesimus felt a peculiar mix of emotions. Gratitude for Paulus' foresight, love for the man who was his spiritual father, and grief at parting from him—perhaps forever—all vied for first place in Onesimus' soul. "Then I will take my leave tomorrow morning. It will be good to finally be able to set things aright," Onesimus nodded. "I had thought to go overland, but I've decided I shall return the way I came; by way of the sea. That way I can make amends along the way as well. I hope God will lead me to the Swan and Captain Alban so I may explain to him and set things on the square."

Paulus laughed a little as he said, "Never you fear! If you need to make amends to anyone the Lord Christ Himself will make certain your paths cross at just the right moment!"

Onesimus laughed in return and nodded. He knew what Paulus had said was true. God always made the necessary possible.

With those thoughts flooding his mind, Onesimus told Paulus he would be back after he found a caravan to travel with and a mount for the trip. Taking denarii from the bag for the horse or mule and needed supplies he would buy, he slipped out the door toward the marketplace where every type of transaction took place on a daily basis.

As he wandered the marketplace he began looking for a horse he could purchase for the trek to Puteoli. He knew that if he were to find a well-equipped caravan, they would not wish to slow their progress for a pedestrian. It wasn't long before he had found two men who had horses for sale. Now, they stood before him, each telling him how magnificent and noble his particular steed was.

Onesimus looked the horses over and, frankly, was not impressed with either one. Fortunately, he wasn't looking for a horse with whom he could have a life-long relationship. He simply wanted something that would last through the nine-day journey to the port.

The first man, a man as tall as himself but weighing about twice as much, took him by the arm and said loudly, "This horse is only four years old. She is sound of wind and will make a fine addition to your stables! Only three hundred denarii!"

The second seller jumped in, "Three hundred denarii! I will *give away* this horse to you for only two hundred and eighty denarii! This fine bay animal has spent all of his life pastured at my compound north of the city. He is a fine four year old who is ready to ride and of a quiet temperament."

Onesimus looked the first man straight in the eye and spoke quietly. "Do you think I do not know horseflesh? Do you think I am a child? I assure you neither is the case. This mare of yours is more like," he spread the horse's lips and looked at the teeth, "more like ten years old. And I would wager her sound wind is more wind sounds! How long has she had the heaves? I couldn't give you more than fifty denarii for this broken down, spavined nag!"

At this, the second candidate started to snicker and Onesimus rounded on him. "You haven't any room to judge seeing that your gelding is," again Onesimus spread the lips of the animal in question, "a good six years old and suffers from sweet itch!" He pointed to the severe rash surrounding the horse's tail. "I am willing to give you one hundred denarii; more for the sake of the horse than for my sake. Hopefully a change of stable will help clear this problem up."

Onesimus wasn't pretending to know horses. He had spent many happy hours in the horse stables near his home when he was a boy. The hostlers there had taken a liking to the intelligent, loving lad and had taught him much about horses and their care. He truly did feel sorry for the horse with sweet itch. He knew it came more to horses who spent time in poorly cared-for stables than those that were kept clean. He was hoping the man would agree to the paltry sum so he could take care of the horse and see him healed.

As for the first horse, he felt sorry for her, too but he knew there was little that could be done to heal the hock that was swollen with a bony growth which would soon bring on a severe lameness. He knew as well that the heaves, a breathing condition that could crop up suddenly with exertion, could never be repaired.

"You can't save all of Greece!" his father used to declare on a regular basis. "You can only save what you can save." This was his father's excuse for his total lack of concern for others of lesser worth, but Onesimus knew that in some ways, his father had been right.

Thrusting the coins forward, Onesimus waited for the horse's owner to spit in his face or take the money, he didn't know which.

The man stared at him for a fleeting second and finally snatched the coins from his hand and gave him the reins. "Good luck to you!" he offered as his departing words.

Onesimus led his horse around the marketplace until he saw a group of people talking together on a side street. He stood and listened for a short time, hoping to learn their plans. They were obviously not close to each other. Some of the women were standing together talking about the children who played around them. Onesimus saw a couple of the men give an abbreviated salute to one another as they were obviously introducing themselves.

"It shouldn't take more than eight days if we are all well-mounted. It may take nine or more if we take on folks who have to walk," he heard a short man say to a woman. "I think we need to refuse any pedestrians just for the sake of time."

"I have an extra mount I could spare for a single person. Why not do that first?" the woman replied.

The man laughed, "You always were a generous person. If you prefer to let a stranger ride your horse to telling them they cannot go with us, fine."

"Excuse me," Onesimus interrupted. "I am looking for a caravan to join to Puteoli. Is that your destination?"

The woman nodded, "That is our general direction although some of us have other destinations."

The man glanced at the horse Onesimus was leading and frowned slightly at the sight of the severe sweet itch rash.

"I just bought him for the trip," Onesimus explained. "Has a little problem with sweet itch, but I'm hoping it will clear up once I get him away from his careless former owner. I am willing to keep him with me instead of with the other horses if you are worried."

"No!" the man said quickly. "I don't think a little sweet itch will be a problem. How about you?" he turned to the woman beside him.

"No. No problem as far as I can see," she answered. "Can you be ready to depart at sunup tomorrow?"

Onesimus nodded. "Of course. I am Onesimus and I look forward to travelling with you."

The man introduced himself as Julian and the woman as his wife Felicity and once more welcomed him to the group. Then Julian introduced him around to the twenty-or-so adults and children that stood in the street.

After giving up on remembering any names, Onesimus took his leave and promised to meet the caravan on the outskirts of the city along the Appian Way at sunup in the morning.

"Remember," Julian called as Onesimus began his ride back to the small house Paulus had rented, "if you aren't here at sunup, you will miss us."

Onesimus nodded and waved, "I'll be here."

CHAPTER TWENTY

I f Onesimus was worried that he would oversleep and miss the caravan he had no need. He tossed all night and when he was able to lose consciousness it was only to jerk awake again after a few minutes to begin the whole process again.

Beyond his food supply, he only had a curry comb for the horse, a cloak and a comb to carry, so he didn't need to pack. In the pre-dawn light, Onesimus took one more tour around the little house he had shared with his spiritual father, teacher and friend. He cut himself a piece of cheese and tore off a chunk of crusty bread for his break fast and ate as he wandered around the little domicile. At last he stood over Paulus' couch and thought of all the things he had learned from him. He wished he'd been able to find the words he needed to express his gratitude. He wished he had more time to continue his spiritual education. He didn't feel ready. He didn't feel he had learned half enough to leave! But he knew he had to go.

"Better be moving along, son," came a quiet voice. "You mustn't miss the caravan."

"You should still be sleeping!" Onesimus protested quietly.

"I'm losing my son to the wide world today. How could I sleep? Let us pray before you leave."

Paulus rose from his pallet and placed both hands on Onesimus' shoulders and began to pray. "Christ Jesus we come to You without a hope except the hope we have in You. You are holy, You are righteous, You are love itself and for my dear friend, I entreat Your protection for his travels, Your wisdom for his decisions and Your will for his life. Thank You, Lord and Savior, that You have allowed me to know this extraordinary young man. Help us to live in the knowledge that, whether we ever see each other in this life again or not, we will be reunited in Your kingdom for eternity. In the name of Christ Jesus, Amen."

No sooner was the "amen" said, than Paulus pulled Onesimus into a bear hug and patted him on the back. "I shall miss you, my friend."

Onesimus returned the embrace and murmured, "And I, you. I know you well enough to know you won't be staying here long now that you are free to go."

Paulus laughed as he led the traveler to the door. "You are right about that. Already I hear a cry for help arising from your destination as well as Miletus and Crete. I am only sending you on ahead of me because you have been gone from your master for long enough. Besides, I have stops to make along the way that would slow your return down. Fare thee well and safe travels."

With that, Onesimus mounted his horse and headed toward the Appian Way and the gates of Rome knowing all along that one pair of loving eyes were watching him all the way to the first turn where he turned in the saddle and waved as he went out of sight.

He arrived outside the gates just before Januarius, Rufina and their family approached from the east. Julian's group was already present and two more groups were slated to come along. Julian waited until a little past sunrise before he began to suggest they be moving along. They were checking pack animals' burdens and tightening harness in preparation to leave when one more late-arriving group of travelers joined them. Directly after that, a boy about six ran through the city gates. He was out of breath and calling out even as he approached the caravan.

Julian, a father himself, knelt down and took the boy by the shoulders, "What is it, Theophilus? Catch your breath and tell me what's afoot."

It took a couple minutes before the boy could speak coherently but the story seemed simple enough when he finally managed it.

"Father told me to tell you," he screwed up his face in an effort to remember word for word the message he had promised his father to deliver. "Mother's miserable father caught word that our family was leaving Rome. He called on Aeolus to raise a violent storm if father insisted on going. Grandfather says no upstart whelp will ever take his daughter away from him!"

Julian did his best to hide the grin that had appeared when he heard that last sentence as he replied. "That's fine. Tell your father we understand and that we thank him for letting us know. Tell him also that we hope he gains his freedom soon."

The boy stood still, nodding as he memorized the message and then he turned and ran back through the gates of the city.

After he had disappeared, Julian turned to Onesimus and explained, "Theophilus' father is definitely in control of his household. His wife is a meek little thing, but her father uses the gods as if they were his personal servants to control everyone around him!"

Onesimus just smiled and shook his head. How long would the people of this city remain in the darkness that allowed that degree of manipulation? How long before they learned of the freedom to be found in the Annointed One?

"Father," he prayed silently. "Help me to somehow be a part of the work that breaks the chains of slavery to false gods!" And he knew that he would start soon with the little group that traveled with him as God would guide him.

CHAPTER TWENTY-ONE

It wasn't long before the small group had completed their organizing and had left the gates of Rome for the Appian Way and the port city of Puteoli.

Onesimus noticed almost immediately that the sounds of this caravan were much different than the sounds he had heard as he entered Rome.

There was no chinking of chains, no grumbled curses, or shuffling of reluctant feet. Instead, he heard the clopping of horses' hooves, the happy shouts of children running and playing together, the murmurs of private conversations peppered with the occasional corrective bellow from a father to his child.

It wasn't long before he became aware of a small, brown-spotted horse trotting along beside him. The mare was ridden by a young girl of about ten years old. As he glanced over her eyes met his and he was struck by the wisdom that shone from her.

"Hello," she said quietly. "I am Julian's daughter, Martina." She glanced down at her small, white hands and back to

Onesimus again. Then she again glanced down at her hands. This time, Onesimus realized that she wanted him to look down as well. He saw at once that she was tracing, over and over, the outline of a fish on the horse's neck.

He tilted his head to one side and raised his eyebrows. "How is it that one so young . . .?"

"My tutor taught me many things for which I shall be forever grateful!" She smiled at him and he smiled and nodded back. Then she moved off to rejoin her family.

Although there were several small towns between Rome and Puteoli the group had decided that camping beside the road whenever the journey became tiresome would make more sense than trekking onward to the next town in hopes of finding some sort of taverna So the group passed through Three Taverns shortly after noon and had moved on; camping by the road when the evening of the first day arrived.

Traveling in caravan with strangers was always a gamble, Onesimus knew. The leader of the caravan could be lazy and shiftless to an outrageous degree, spending hours sitting around during the midday meal and stopping for the night long before sunset. This type would be unwilling to exert the effort to assist a fellow-traveler in trouble.

The other half of the story would be a driver: someone wanting to start exactly at sunrise if not before, eating while on the move and driving the caravan on through the evening until there was not a scintilla of light to see by. This type would hesitate to stop long enough to assist a fellow-traveler in trouble, because it would add length to the journey.

Onesimus was glad to discover that Julian was neither. He traveled from dawn to dusk with a stop at midday for a sensible meal and time for the animals to rest. He didn't hesitate to call an early halt the second day out when Januarius's second son twisted his ankle and had to be cosseted by his mother for a short time. Then the group forged on.

Just as they were well underway again, they were startled by a shout from behind them. They halted their progress and turned to see a man trotting toward them on the road. He was carrying a pack and, though dust-covered, was well-dressed and didn't look like a robber, so the little band waited patiently until the round little fellow reached them.

"Oh! Hello! I was so happy to see you passing! I was on my way to Capua yesterday when my horse lamed up. Since it was late in the day I decided to clear the pebble and let him rest overnight before continuing. Unfortunately, he has developed a fever in his leg and I can't very well ride him like that, so I was hoping you would allow me to travel with you. I could ride in the cart with the children, if you don't mind."

Julian, who prided himself in being a good judge of character, nevertheless looked at the rest of the group to gather a consensus. Seeing nods from several, he agreed to allow the stranger to join their company.

Scrambling into the cart, the traveler said, "Ah! Yes! My name is Malchus. I am most grateful!" He wiped his brow and balding head with a cloth from his pocket. The gesture left a muddy streak of dust and sweat behind which no one pointed out to him. He seemed to have had enough troubles.

It was shortly after Malchus joined them that Onesimus realized they were passing the place where the guard's horse had fallen. The events of that day, although almost two years gone, were still powerful and clear in Onesimus' mind. He turned to Julian who rode beside him and spoke, "I've a story to tell which you may or may not believe. Nevertheless I assure you every word is true. Would you like to hear it?" At Julian's nod, he recounted the story of the miraculous healing of a guard's horse.

Onesimus was so skillful in the telling that Julian almost saw the horse stepping in the hole and going down, the broken pastern swelling so rapidly you could watch it happening. He heard the tortured sound of the horse's huffing breath and saw Paulus quietly doing God's bidding. The snorting of the horse as he struggled to his feet was easy to imagine and the soldiers' gasping at the sight of this "dumb animal" being healed by the intervention of one of their prisoners was heard in Julian's imagination. Julian easily imagined the guard replacing his short sword in its scabbard as he was unashamedly wiping tears from his face and then grabbing Paulus in a bear hug as he repeated over and over, "Thank you! Thank you! I am indebted to you!"

Shaking his head, Julian was silent for a moment after the account was finished.

"You're saying this man, this prisoner on the way to Caesar, was able to heal a horse's broken leg just by touching him? That *is* hard to believe, my friend."

"Well," Onesimus explained. "It really wasn't the man ... it was the God he serves that did the healing. I had already seen him pray to his God about a fellow-prisoner with open sores and watched those sores heal. I knew that his God was capable of healing but, as one guard said, 'Humans are one thing but I can't believe his God is going to care about a dumb animal!'

"The funny thing about this whole event was the fact that the guards who had seen the prisoner pray for the healing of his fellow prisoner had started to believe it was some sort of magic act; that Paulus had somehow faked the whole episode. When the horse fell, the swelling of his leg was immediate and visible to all. And when the horse stood up and walked away, carrying his owner on his back, that too was visible to all! It is fair hard to accuse a horse of collusion, my friend!" Onesimus laughed.

Julian nodded his head slightly. "Yes. I've heard stories of these types of things among the new cult that has been growing in Rome lately." The nod became a slight sideways shake, "But I've never seen it. While I have no doubt at all that you are an honest man who believes you saw that horse healed, I'm afraid until I see it myself I will continue to have doubts about these so-called *miracles*. My own daughter's tutor talks about these things but ..."

"Never mind! I've lived a long time without ever seeing a miracle and I do not believe *anyone* has ever seen a true miracle!" came a loud comment from the cart. "I do not believe in miracles, gods or any other of the fairy tales our parents and the priests and priestesses have fed us over the years."

"I understand what you are saying, friend," replied Onesimus. "But I know what I saw and I will pray that you will see something similar that you cannot argue against.

"Meanwhile, rest your mind that I do not believe in the 'gods and other fairy tales' our parents fed us, either. I believe in a single God; the God who created everything and who loved us enough to die for us!"

When he realized what he was saying, Onesimus wished he could reach out and pull those words back into his mouth. Yet, he realized that God might be using them to pique the interest of his listeners.

"So . . .," Malchus hissed. "You are one of those *Christians* who have caused so much trouble! Tell me, do you really eat the flesh of your god *and* of your children during your meetings?"

Several of the women began to chatter loudly, trying to stave off what might very well become a physical confrontation, but Onesimus knew he had to finish what his story had started.

He sucked in a big breath and then closed his eyes. He spoke quietly when he replied, "No. We do not eat the flesh of our God. We eat a fellowship meal and then we take bread and wine as a remembrance of what He did for us."

For a while after that the only sound in the group was the clopping of hooves, the children chattering together and the adults discussing their plans for dinner and where they should stop for the night. But Onesimus noticed that Martina was watching him.

That evening, while Januarius was seeing to his animals, Julian suggested to the women that it might be better to have everyone contribute food for the evening meal and have a single meal prepared for everyone by the women. The women immediately began shaking their heads.

"Absolutely not!" Felicity declared. "First, it wasn't planned that way, so the food contributed probably wouldn't mix well for a meal. Second each family is familiar with mother's own cooking style and a group meal means that no one would truly be happy with the meals prepared and third, I'm certain that Rufina will agree with me that neither of us is ready to cook for seventeen people every night after traveling all day!"

Throughout this vehement refusal, Rufina was standing off to the side, arms crossed, shaking her head. Onesimus had to hide his grin when he saw Julian raise both hands shoulder height and shake his head side to side as he responded, "All right. I'm sorry I thought of it. I won't mention it again." He dropped to his knees, "Please, *please* forgive me. I didn't know I was asking for the impossible. I'm sorry!" By this time, Felicity had begun chuckling and soon everyone was laughing including Rufina, Felicity, Julian, and Onesimus.

As the group began to bed down for the evening, Onesimus wondered how close they were to where the wolves had attacked the prisoners' caravan. As he looked upward, he whispered a prayer of thanks to God that he had been able to clarify a common horrible libel against the people of God as well as plant a seed within the breast of his new friend. He prayed that God would send someone to water and someone to harvest at the proper times.

From there, the prayer changed course and became a prayer for the safety of the caravan and the protection of all his fellow-travelers, followed by a prayer of praise and joy that the God of Israel was now his God.

Soon after concluding his prayer Onesimus drifted into a deep, peaceful sleep that lasted until the rustling of his fellow nomads awakened him at first light.

CHAPTER
TWENTY-TWO

The caravan had traveled only about two leagues when Onesimus glanced ahead and recognized the clearing where the wolves had caused such an upset in the camp that night so long ago.

So far the day's travel had been relatively quiet, so to lighten their day's journey Onesimus thought he might tell the tale to those who traveled with him.

"On the seventh day of my journey to Rome, our caravan set up camp right up there," he pointed to the clearing. "Several of my companions complained it was too close to the road and that the surrounding shrubbery and trees gave too much cover for enemies but the Captain of the Guards insisted, so camp was established.

"Everything seemed to go well and it wasn't long before we were all wrapped in our cloaks and preparing for sleep.

"I had just begun to drift off when my friend, Paulus, raised himself on his elbow and told me he heard something in the brush. He wanted me to listen too. It was only a moment when I heard what he was talking about. The hair on the back of my neck stood up when I heard the sound of the brush rustling. Several birds were roused enough to take off from the surrounding trees. Something or someone was certainly trying to sneak into the camp.

"'Wolves!' Paulus whispered, and when I looked closely I too could see four pair of golden eyes, blinking and moving quietly toward the guards' resting place.

"All the guards had drifted into slumber except for the watch who sat near the road and who was paying no attention to the underbrush surround the camp.

"Without thinking, or discussing it, both Paulus and I quickly sat up at the same time shouting and making enough noise to raise Tiberias, himself! Of course, the whole camp erupted in an uproar and the guards were just about ready to beat the two of us.

"At first, when we tried to explain we had seen wolves creeping toward the guards they didn't believe us. It didn't help that the watch decided he had to protect himself and declared he had not seen anything. He falsely averred that he had made circuit of the camp just before the alarm was sounded. Finally, when the Captain of the Guards used a torch he found the paw prints. The encampment calmed their thirst for revenge long enough to hear him confirm our story. He showed them all the paw prints in the dirt.

"After *that* experience, I would urge us to move on even if it were the middle of the night!" Onesimus nodded emphatically and the others were quiet for a while wondering why wolves would venture so close to the road in a season when game would have been plentiful.

Julian was especially skeptical and advanced toward the campsite where he suddenly stopped his horse. "I'm wondering if those wolves are still around! I'm going to go look over there and see if I can see any prints or other evidence of wolves in the area."

Felicity called to him, "Julian, please don't! If there *are* wolves . . ."

Julian called back to her, "It's all right. Wolves are afraid of humans. They won't attack a human unless they are starving and this is the wrong time of year for that!"

"Do be cautious," Onesimus called. "It was the wrong time of year when they came into our camp, too."

Julian laughed a little and Onesimus gazed through the heat-wrinkled air as the scoffer reached the clearing and started peering at the ground. At one point, he knelt down and stared intently at something he saw on the ground. He started to rise and then seemed to freeze. Slowly, he raised his head and looked toward the bushes then he *slowly* turned his head and looked toward the caravan. Onesimus could swear the man's face was the color of wool that had been washed with fuller's soap.

Onesimus kicked his horse into action and headed for the clearing at a gallop. As he went he kept shouting, "Hey! Heee Haaaa! Hey! hey! hey!"

Bursting from the bushes, a wolf flew past Julian and crossed the clearing at a run, disappearing into the woods on the far side.

A second later, Julian was standing at his side. His voice shook as he said, "Thank you, friend. I am so glad you understood what I was thinking! Forever I will ponder the mystery of well-fed wolves that attack humans in summer and remember the man who rescued me from certain doom!"

Julian was standing out of sight on the far side of the horse from the caravan so only Onesimus saw him reach out and grab the saddle's belly strap as his knees buckled and he almost fell.

As they returned to the caravan, Felicity came up to Julian and, standing with arms akimbo, shouted at him. "Always having to see for yourself!" she shouted. "Do you see what that almost got you?" She slugged his chest with her fists and shouted, "You stupid, stupid man! You scared me to death! OOOOOH! You stupid man!" she broke into her own tirade with weeping, "Oh! If it hadn't been for Onesimus' quick thinking, you would have been eaten and I would be widowed and... and... *I love you!*" She threw her arms around his neck and clung to him just as ivy clings to a wall.

Julian put his arms around her and comforted her for a minute, murmuring apologies and petting her back.

Shortly, the emotional storm passed and the caravan was on its way again, but Onesimus quickly decided to not tell any more tales of his adventures to his fellow-travelers. It was too dangerous.

It was late afternoon when the travelers reached the market town of the Forum of Appius. While Onesimus was being very mindful of the fact that all the money he carried was rightfully Philemon's, others seemed to have plenty to spend on fresh food and even a few pieces of clothing. Remembering that Paulus told him to use what he needed and Philemon would receive recompense from Paulus when he arrived, Onesimus did spend a few sestertii on fresh bread and enough roasted goat for a single meal.

The trip through this town took a little longer than usual because of the purchases being made, but overall it didn't take as long as it could have. Onesimus, as well as Julian, was grateful for that.

By the time the caravan had traveled a league outside the town the sun was setting and it was time to settle down for the night. They found a sandy place beside a deep stream and tethered their horses near the water. Breaking out their provisions, they sat around eating and talking for a short time. No one noticed how quiet Malchus was.

What happened next was never quite clear to most of the observers of the event... nor was it really clear to Onesimus.

Onesimus had put away his leftovers and had taken his cloak off to wrap around himself for the night when Malchus spoke.

"I understand you followers of the Jewish God not only eat the flesh of your god, but you also kill children and roast them for supper! Is this true? AHHH! I shouldn't bother asking you! You will just lie about it anyway. I have a good friend whose uncle's neighbor's hired hand went to one of your meetings. He told me himself that this fellow *saw* a child roasting on a spit! You need to die!"

With this, he launched himself across the clearing at Onesimus and swung a dagger at Onesimus' throat. Onesimus stepped sideways as his attacker flew at him. The knife slicing through his forearm left a path of searing heat but did no serious damage.

Malchus, thrown off balance by Onesimus' unpredicted shift, landed firmly in the dying fire Onesimus had built to warm himself. In no more than a second Malchus' fine toga was engulfed in flames and the bystanders' ears were filled with the screams of the angry attacker as the fine linen clothing he wore seemed to turn to flames and drip from his body.

Malchus seemed paralyzed by pain and fear. He lay where he fell and shrieked until Onesimus shook off his shock and fell to his knees beside the human torch, rolling him from the fire and into the surrounding sandy soil. Disregarding the blistering of his own hands, he tried throwing sand on the would-be attacker but when he realized he couldn't cover the man fast enough to smother the flames, he began beating at the flaming cloth with his bare hands. In a couple minutes, Julian joined him in his endeavors, using a saddle blanket and together they managed to smother the flames.

When the flames were out, Julian spread the blanket on the ground and said, "Quickly! Help me get him to the water!" Together, the men rolled the burned and screaming man onto the saddlecloth and carried him to the water's edge. There they waded into the water and lowered him until all of Malchus' already badly blistered body was submerged except for his head.

Onesimus who was carrying the end of the blanket where the moaning man's head was, carefully moved his left hand to a point on the blanket directly above Malchus' head and used his right hand to dip water from the stream and cool his attacker's face and hair. While Malchus' hair wasn't badly burned, it was singed and let off a smell that would forever afterward evoke the memory of flame and smoke and screams for Onesimus.

As he laid his water-filled hand on Malchus' head, Onesimus also took the chance to pray for his unsuspected enemy. "Christ Jesus, You who gave Your life for all those who will believe in You, I would that You not lay to his charge this action Malchus has performed against me. You have taught us that whatsoever sins we remit on earth shall be remitted in Heaven, so I forgive him and I ask You to draw him to You. Remove the pain of these burns and heal him right now. I ask this by the authority You give to all believers, Amen."

He had no more than finished his prayer when Julian and Malchus both gasped. Onesimus glanced down at the man whose seconds before was a mass of angry blisters and saw that the blisters were gone.

"Let me down!" Malchus was saying. "Don't touch me! Who *are* you? I have never seen anything like this!"

Onesimus lowered the blanket into the water so Malchus could sit up and find his feet. After he had clambered upright, Malchus climbed the bank of the stream and stood staring at Onesimus. Fear of a man who could heal a burned body in a second warred with gratitude for pride of place on his face.

As Onesimus and Julian climbed the small cliff, Onesimus spoke quietly to both of the men. "I did not heal you, Malchus, my God ... the God of the Jews ... did. This was done that you might see and believe."

Onesimus glanced from Julian to Malchus as they headed into the center of the camp. "When you have thought about this experience and what you have seen, let me know and we will talk again."

He patted Malchus and Julian on their shoulders and moved off to wrap in his cloak and sleep until morning.

Upon awakening, Onesimus was startled to find three of the women standing around him with what could only be described as "offerings" to him. Felicity and another held fresh bread and cooked eggs while the third held a beautiful bouquet of wildflowers.

The minute his eyes met their eyes they knelt down and offered up their gifts.

Shocked, he shook his head and spoke firmly, "No! Do not bow to me. I am only a man and do not want your adoration. If you want to honor the One who healed Malchus last night, then reverence the God I serve, I do not deserve your devotion."

The women insisted he take their gifts but he just as firmly refused until they finally gave up and went back to their own families.

With the exception of a short visit to Terracina, the group moved along at a steady pace for the next two days. Malchus never spoke to Onesimus, but Onesimus often saw him and Julian together. This seeming exclusion didn't bother him because he knew the two of them were considering what they had seen and what they would do with this knowledge.

The clopping of the horses' hooves and their occasional nickering and huffing were familiar and soothing. The children's piping voices were often heard asking questions of Malchus, who rode with them. The idea of an adult riding with them (and one who had nearly died in front of their eyes, at that!) fascinated them and, in turn, Malchus had a fine time answering all their questions . . . whether he knew the answer or not. The only changes in the journey came with the changing sights, sounds, and aromas.

Perhaps the scent of roasting fish or baking bread would tease the hungry travelers as they passed a dwelling beside the road. Sometimes, (perhaps more than "some" times), the odors weren't as pleasant as the travelers would pass the contents of a dumped slops jar or an animal that had died by the road.

On their journey the travelers could see and experience many different things. They might see and smell a field of flowers. Once, they passed a man who was an obvious lunatic standing by the road, swinging his arms erratically and shouting in panic, "Don't let them get me! They're trying to kill me! Help! Help!" The travelers could do nothing to help him. It was obvious that there was nothing there to defend against. The man's enemies were not of this world but of his tortured mind.

Because every adult, except Malchus, was mounted and the children and Malchus rode in the cart pulled by a donkey most of the time, the caravan made much better time than the incoming prisoners' convoy had.

By the afternoon of the sixth day out, boredom was beginning to take a toll. The children were quarrelling and the adults were testy. It seemed as if even the food had conspired against the little band. In Onesimus' case it seemed as if the food consisted of bread and cheese in the morning and cheese and bread in the evening with a choice of bread or cheese at the midday. It didn't help that Rufina had opened a small barrel of salted fish and found that it had gone bad in the summer heat.

While he was brooding about this, praying that they would see a vendor who would have something delicious to sell, one of Januarius' boys who was always darting off the side of the road into the surrounding fields to explore, came running back to the group. His face was covered in juice and he held his hands out in front of him filled with tiny red berries.

"Look! Look!" he shouted with the pride of one who has provided for his family, "I found these over there by the rock wall!"

Januarius jumped from his horse and looked closely at what the boy was holding.

"Heart berries!" he called to the group. "The boy has found some wild heart berries." He turned to Julian. "Let's stay long enough to gather some."

At Julian's nod, everyone left their horses and headed over to the wall where the juicy heartberries hid among their leaves. It didn't take long for everyone to find enough fruit to satisfy their longing for something fresh and sweet and the small procession was soon on its way again; but with everyone in a much better mood.

That evening the mood was further lifted when Julian announced, "Friends, you will be happy to know we are within a day's travel of the city of Capua, where some of us will leave the Appian Way to travel overland to Puteoli!"

Excitement reigned for the next few minutes as horses were fed and curried, children were collected, fed and bedded down and the adults fixed and ate their evening repasts.

It came as no surprise to Onesimus when together, Julian and Malchus approached him after supper, when the fires were dying down.

"When you did what you did back there at the creek," Malchus began, "I thought you had put a hex on me. While I wasn't *afraid* I was . . . mmm . . . *startled*. That's it. I was startled.

"But Julian and I have been talking about it and we have discussed your story about the healed horse and we agree. We would like to hear more about this Anointed One you spoke to. This . . . Christ . . . that you say did the healing of my burns. Please . . . tell us about him."

With heart lifting, Onesimus threw a few more sticks on his fire and began, "It was about thirty or forty years ago that a young Jew began proclaiming the Kingdom of God. He soon had raised quite a following and had revealed Himself to His followers to be the very Son of the God of Israel, but for some time He warned them to not reveal this fact to anyone outside the group . . ."

CHAPTER
TWENTY-THREE

The seventh day of the journey dawned cloudy but dry and those who had traveled under a brilliant Roman sun for six days rejoiced in the relief the heavy cloud cover provided. It wasn't long before they had started out toward Capua and the parting of the ways where those going to Puteoli would leave the Appian Way and would travel over the hills and down to that port city on the Bay of Naples.

As they reached the outskirts of Capua in mid-afternoon the weary wayfarers decided to have a little celebration. Januarius and Rufina went on into town to gather some fresh fruit and meat while Julian, Onesimus, and Malchus stayed behind to tend the horses and built a fire with a spit.

The couple returned carrying pomegranates, pears, turnips, onions and a lamb ready for the spit. When the lamb and vegetables were roasting together over the fire and everyone had completed their tasks for the evening Januarius revealed that he was a fine lutist by breaking out his bull and tortoise lute. Rufina soon appeared with an aulos to accompany her husband and dancing and merriment broke out all over the camp.

"Friends!" Julian called after the sun had set and the scent of roasting lamb had made every mouth in the camp water with anticipation. "I do believe this wonderful celebration has reached its zenith! My wife tells me the lamb is ready and we may gather round to enjoy the finest meal prepared this journey!"

The trek was completed for Malchus, who was going to visit his brother in Capua. Januarius, Rufina and their children were taking the Aemilia Scaura Way, continuing their trip to Rufina's hometown of Rhegium. The other couple was traveling on down the Appian Way to the town of Brundisium located in the "heel of Italy". That left Julian, Felicity and their children, and Onesimus to travel overland to Puteoli where Julian's parents lived.

Only Onesimus would be traveling onward from Puteoli and, in some ways, he was glad of that. He would be able to spend a little time seeing Puteoli and finding out if or when the Swan was due to arrive. He felt an intense compulsion to talk with Captain Alban so he could set that part of his past straight.

The journey's end celebration lasted for several hours, allowing the travelers to reassure themselves that their trek together really was coming to an end. Even so, by the time the moon was high overhead the festivities had concluded and the weary group had found their beds for the night. The only noises to be heard were the quiet murmurings of those who were still awake and stentorian snores emanating from the area of Malchus' bed.

Onesimus smiled to himself, remembering the past week. His struggles with Malchus' prejudices and the joy of leading him to the Savior, his memories of traveling this route with Paulus, his quiet assurance that Julian and Felicity were considering the miracles they had witnessed themselves and those he had recounted to them. He had a quiet certainty that someone else would come along to water the seeds he had planted.

With these thoughts filling his mind, Onesimus drifted into a deep and peaceful sleep. The kind of sleep he had enjoyed regularly since Yeshua had changed the direction of his life.

Departure day dawned in a steady down-drizzle of warm rain. Although the rain was almost a mist rather than rain it still made it impossible to build a fire so most of the group settled for bread and cheese to break their fast.

Onesimus was not a rain-lover. If he had been on his own, he would have tried to find somewhere to shelter until the following day, but he knew that Julian and Felicity were eager to travel onward. He also knew that the larger the traveling party, the less likely it was that they would be set upon by brigands. As a lone traveler, Onesimus would be the most likely target for attack. If he traveled on with his companions today, his presence would add size to Julian's family and, consequently, would create an increased measure of protection for them all.

Julian, Felicity, their children, and Onesimus were the last to leave the campsite, close on the heels of Januarius and his family. By day's end, the little crowd that was headed to the port city would have reached their destination, but Januarius and Rufina would still have several days' journey ahead of them.

Onesimus reflected that the leave-taking hadn't gone as he had thought it would. There were no long good-byes, salutes and pats on the back when all were ready to leave. Instead, each party simply gathered their things and moved off in the direction they were going. It was as if the real separation had taken place during the celebration the night before.

For Onesimus and Julian's family, the leaving simply consisted of making certain all the children were accounted for and then a right turn onto a path heading west to the coast . . . to the port town of Puteoli . . . Julian to his parents' Puteoli home and Onesimus on to the rest of his life, however long or short it would be.

Chapter Twenty-Four

I am certain!" Julian insisted. "Come with us. I know my parents would be happy to let you stay the night. It's much too cold and wet to spend camped out tonight and they have plenty of room!"

Onesimus was hesitant to barge into the home of complete strangers and ask for shelter, but it *was* miserably wet and wretchedly cold; and it was late. No doubt he could find shelter for a price at one of the tavernae in the area. But even if he did, there would be no way to dry his clothing or other personal items.

Almost as if he could hear what Onesimus was thinking, Julian continued, "There is room in the kitchen to spread out your clothing so it will be dry in the morning. I'm sure that the servants have been instructed to keep the fires burning tonight. Knowing my father, he has been working outside most of the day and needs to dry his own clothing. Please come."

Without much more thought, Onesimus found himself nodding in agreement and abandoning the roadway that led toward the quay for a smaller, quieter passage that led in a northerly direction to Julian's family homestead located just beyond the first rise.

True to Julian's prediction, his mother welcomed him almost as if he were her long-lost son. She clucked over his sorry state, loaned him a few items of clothing to get him through the night and insisted on taking care of his wet things without help. She was so solicitous, he half-expected her to reach out and ruffle his hair.

As soon as everyone was dry and comfortable, she called a servant in and ordered up a warm supper of leftover roasted doves with artichokes and calda, a drink made of spiced warm water and wine. The supper was a welcome feast for the travelers and, as they ate, the hosts shared all the local news with their son and his family and friend.

It wasn't long before the children had settled into sleep without complaint, content just to have reached their destination and to be out of the rain and resting on real couches instead of the ground.

"I had the worst time with Pamphilus's horse!" Julian's father sighed as he settled onto his couch for the evening. "First thing I noticed when he was brought to me the other day was that Pamphilus had been too distracted to realize the poor fellow's horse sandal had broken until he started to go lame. Some idiot stressed the metal until it was brittle and it cracked. I made Pamphilus take the horse home to rest him and bring him back the next day. When he got back yesterday I found that when I touched his foot to prepare it for the new sandal that pitiable horse would jerk and start away. It was obviously still very tender. I asked Pamphilus what he had done and he admitted he had ridden that unfortunate horse home because 'it was too far to walk!' I kept the horse overnight last night to save him from the walk, *and* his owner, and finally managed to get him quieted enough to replace the shoe today. Now that ignorant fool doesn't want to pay me for the extra time and effort I took to save his horse!"

"So then, it wasn't really the horse you had the hard time with, right?" Julian asked with a smile. "It was Pamphilus who was the problem!"

His father nodded in agreement. "You're right about that! Some people are just too stupid to be allowed to have horses!"

"And speaking of horses," he turned toward Onesimus. "I noticed your mount was in pretty good shape for a ten-year-old."

"Hmm!" Onesimus responded. "I bought him in Rome and I'm certain he's six, not ten."

"Ah! No! He's ten if he's a day. I understand you're getting ready to sail off to Greece, and what are you going to do with that animal?"

Cutting his glance toward Julian and grinning widely Onesimus replied, "Oh! I thought I'd just take him into town and see what I could get for him. Now that his sweet itch is cleared up I might be able to raise fifty denarii for him."

"Oh, now!" Julian's father rejoined. "You obviously shouldn't be allowed out into the streets alone yet! You could easily get seventy five denarii for him. He's a gelding, to be sure, but even so, he has several good years left. In fact, I would be more than willing to give you . . . one hundred denarii for him! Is it a deal?"

Onesimus again glanced at Julian who had heard Onesimus talk enough about horses to know that he knew horses and knew he could probably get two hundred denarii in the local marketplace. Even so, Onesimus agreed to the *generous* offer of one hundred denarii, knowing that that amount would replace what he had paid for the steed and that was all he truly cared about. Besides, the generosity of this giving family had impressed him mightily and he wished to give back as much as possible.

After shaking hands on the deal, everyone retired to their couches where they slept through the night and the thunderstorm that struck after the moon had set.

A blade of bright sunshine stabbed through the windows and moved rapidly across the marble floor of the salon where Onesimus slept creeping up the body on the couch until it poked and prodded at the closed eyes of the couch's occupant.

Groaning, Onesimus threw his arm over his eyes and tried to pretend he wasn't awake but it was too late. His brain knew better even if his bones and muscles ached to stay absent. He finally gave up and sat up. After a few moments to adjust to an upright position, he rose from the couch, staggering across the salon like a drunken man in search of a drink.

"Good! You're awake!"

The cheerful voice only made Onesimus feel worse. How could anyone be that cheerful this early in the day?

"I've got your money, here. The morning meal has been served and you need to get to table if you want anything. Julian has an appetite as huge as your horse's! There is a fine dish of eggs and cheese and a bit of cold dove left from last night. There is also libae. You know; those fine, small rolls that melt on your tongue."

While the thundering tones of Julian's father was grating on ears that were barely awake Onesimus reflected that they did the trick of getting one awake and moving. He nodded silently to the man and moved toward the table where he could see laid out all the delicious things he had heard described.

It wasn't long and breakfast was in the past and Onesimus was on his way, walking along with his stolen bag of coins and the 100 denarii he had gotten for his horse secreted beneath his girdle. He topped the rise above Julian's home and stopped, stunned by the sight below him. Two-masted warships and single-sailed merchant ships jostled for elbow room in the harbor below. The sun scattered stars across water that flashed and sparked in the eyes of the beholder.

He only had a short walk to the city center where he could begin to search for a ship heading to Colossae and for the Swan. He could only pray that he would find both under the command of the kindly Captain Alban.

Soon enough he was standing by the docks, listening to the familiar bustle and busy-ness of the crowded seaport. Above the sounds of loading and unloading, the shouting and cursing of the sailors and captains, and the thumping of ships against the piers Onesimus could hear a strange cacophony of sounds he couldn't identify. There were roars and bellows, grunts and hisses the likes of which he had never heard before.

He followed the sounds toward one area of the docks where he could see a grouping of crates of different sizes. As he approached he smelled a tremendous odor that was reminiscent of a badly kept stable. The sounds grew louder until he was close enough to see what the crates contained.

Animals. There were giant cats that looked just like the lions that were carved into various buildings around Rome. There were other cats that had yellow and black stripes, and one crate contained a horse that was covered from head to hoof with black and white stripes!

As he stood looking through the bars of the crates, a voice called out, "Here! Don't get too near to some of 'em! They bites and they claws, they do! Fascinatin' though, ain't they? Bound for Caesar's circus, they are!"

Onesimus looked up to see a sailor who looked familiar. Just like the fellow who had taught him how to splice lines on Captain Alban's ship.

"Joannes?" he asked incredulously. "Is that really you?"

The sailor closed one eye and tilted his head as he stared at Onesimus. "Zacheus? Salve! Thought you was long gone, I did. Thought I'd never see the likes o' ye agin! How have ya been? How'd your Roman business go?"

Onesimus laughed. "Friend, my Roman business went better than I could have imagined. In fact, I am now headed back to Ephesus to take care of the business I left undone there!"

"You're a busy man! If your business can wait a short time, we will be heading toward Ephesus in about a week."

"I was hoping you would tell me that, Joannes. I have the time to wait and I have to have a discussion with Captain Alban, if possible. Is he aboard?"

"Ay! He be right over there where the crates came from! I'll see you aboard if not before."

Onesimus reached out and took his friend by the arm. "No. I need to set something straight with you as well."

Joannes's eyes narrowed as he wondered why he was being detained.

"Nothing terribly wrong, friend. I only need to set my paths straight with you. You know me as Zacheus, a businessman from Ephesus. I am really Onesimus, a runaway slave from Colossae."

"What?" Joannes exclaimed. "What do you mean?"

Onesimus' heart was pounding as he continued slowly. "When I bought passage on the Swan I was running away from my master, an olive grower, in Colossae. I had only worked for him for a short time when he found that he was missing some of his olive oil. He suspected me of taking it to sell myself. It wasn't true, but knowing the consequences for a slave accused of theft could be death, I stole enough money to get away and I ran.

"I didn't stop to think that this was a Godly man; a man devoted to his God who taught love and understanding. I didn't stop to think that he had taken me into his home, had treated me fairly, had fed and clothed me with the same things he consumed. Instead, I could only think of the worst possible results of this accusation. So, I ran."

Joannes tilted his head to one side and peered at Onesimus. "I can hardly believe this of you! Why do you tell me these things?"

Onesimus shook his head. "I tell you because in my journeys I met a man who also believed in this God of my master. He told me things and taught me and now, I believe too. That means I need to set all my paths straight starting with you and Captain Alban. Then I need to sail back to Ephesus and travel on to Colossae to my master's house, where I pray he will have mercy on me and will take me back after I tell him everything I have done and ask his forgiveness."

"Oy!" Joannes growled. "I wish you well, Zac--Onesimus! I've no idea how the Cap'n will react to this tale, but I do wish you . . ."

"Zacheus?!" he was interrupted by a feminine voice. "Zacheus is that you?"

Turning toward the voice, Onesimus was surprised to see Philomena standing before him. He smiled and gave a little bow. "It most certainly is, Philomena, and yet it isn't. I am amazed to find you here, in Puteoli! Have you left Ephesus for good, then?"

"No," came the reply. "I'm only here for a season. My great friend, Crispina, sent me a message asking me to come to her aid as she is suffering from a strange illness. She, too, is a childless widow, although her husband was kinder to her than mine was to me. Since she has no one else, I felt obliged to come help her.

"Now, what did you mean it is yet it isn't you, Zacheus?"

Onesimus smiled and began to explain his story once again.

Joannes, having heard the story murmured his hope that Onesimus would voyage with them and moved on about his business.

"I am of a certainty the man you know as Zacheus" he began. "However, my true name is Onesimus." He took her arm and led her to a nearby packing box with room for both of them to sit. There, with the sounds of the sailors, the ships, the tides and the cargos setting up a hubbub around them, he explained to her what he had told to Joannes, and he found that with every telling the inner clamor that had been within him since his run began lessened and peace of soul became more real.

However, while he began to experience more peace, Philomena did not take his confession well.

"How could you lie to me that way, Zacheus... uhh... whatever your name is!" She cried. "I took you into my home and gave you a place to stay, food to eat, and you told me lie after lie! I cannot believe I accepted you for who and what you said you were!" She rose from her seat and began to walk away from him.

"Wait!" Onesimus jumped from his perch and stood in front of her. He continued as she began searching for a way around him, "You are right. I lied to you and I am heartily sorry that I did. But, you must understand that I am not the same man I was then!"

"And why should I believe THAT?" She returned with a vigor borne of betrayal.

"Because I am. I have found the Truth! *Real* Truth! And real truth brooks no falsehood." There was silence for about a minute as Philomena searched the eyes of her betrayer. Then Onesimus continued, "The truth is found not in a philosophy or a cult but only in the bringer of truth, Christ Jesus. He Himself said that He was the Way, the Truth and the Life. And," he continued, "that no one came to know the God of the Universe until they came to know Him."

"There are gods upon gods!" Philomena argued. "What makes you think *your* God is any different than Zeus or Mars?"

Onesimus was quiet a moment.

"Did you not say your friend had a mysterious illness?" He asked.

Philomena nodded, her forehead wrinkling with concern. "Yes," she said. "And I am afraid it will prove to be her last illness! No one can find a cure and she coughs and coughs. She vomits whenever she eats and her fever goes very high at night. Then it plunges downward and her bedclothes become soaked with her sweat. She has pain all over her body at times and then the pain goes away. She says it feels as if she is on fire. I'm so afraid for her!" she said quietly.

Onesimus took Philomena by the hand and said, "Show me where she is. If my God will heal her, will you then believe me and accept that He is the God of the Universe?"

Philomena tilted her head to one side and peered up at him. "I don't believe there is any hope, but if you can heal her I will trust you again!"

"But, dear friend," Onesimus corrected. "It isn't that *I* can do anything, but my God! And trusting me isn't as important as trusting Him."

She reached up in that habitual gesture and shoved her hairdo back into place. "This way!" she said and started off.

Entering the home of Philomena's friend, Onesimus was assaulted with the smell. It smelled of sickness and sadness. Sweaty bedclothes and vomit mingled their odors and created an air of hopelessness.

Spying Philomena's friend lying on a couch he went quickly to her bedside and took her hand. He began to talk with her, asking if she had heard of the God of Israel, asking her if she knew about the sacrifice Jesus had made of His own life, asking her if she wanted to be healed.

Too weak to speak loudly, she spoke in a whisper and said she had never heard but she was willing to learn and to become a disciple of Jesus if He could and would heal her.

Onesimus smiled at her and began to pray. It wasn't a long and elaborate prayer but a simple, "Father, You created this body and I believe I am here to show Your power, grace and mercy to my friends that they might believe on You. Take the fevers, chills and pain away from Crispina and heal her body completely. For the sake of Christ Jesus, I ask it."

Crispina gasped and sat up.

"It's gone! I know it's gone! The pain has disappeared and I feel well!"

Philomena ran across the room and threw herself down on the edge of her friend's couch. Reaching out, she touched the formerly fevered forehead. She looked up at Onesimus and smiled widely. Shoving her hair back into place again, she shook her head and said, "Friend. Tell us more!"

Onesimus smiled first at Crispina and then at a stunned Philomena. "I will be staying in town until the Swan sails for Ephesus at the end of the week. I will gladly teach you every day until I cannot stay to teach you anymore, then you can learn about this teaching from anyone who displays this symbol," here; he drew an ichthus. "These are the followers of this Anointed One and will welcome you at any time. I will be back later today to talk to you more about my God."

He nodded and turned to leave, picking up his pack as he stepped through the door.

CHAPTER
TWENTY-FIVE

Face-to-face with Onesimus, Captain Alban peered into the eyes of his would-be crewman. He had just heard the sorry tale Onesimus had to tell and was perfectly still; thinking. A line appeared between his brows as he stood there and his eyes narrowed considerably. Onesimus was afraid to hear what the Captain would say and yet he knew that God had everything under control.

Several seconds passed before, finally, the Captain's eyes slowly closed and opened again. A slow blink, another, and another. "I've never heard such a tale in my life! I've heard of a lot of runaways but I've never heard of one returning to the place they ran from! I certainly can't understand your motivation! Why, boy, you could be headed directly into a Nor'easter that'll wipe ye from the face of the earth! You know that, don't ye?"

Onesimus nodded silently. He knew, but he had no more to say until he was able to determine what the Captain's ultimate reaction to his confession would be.

"And yer goin' back now to make things right with yer master? How you gonna do that? If yer a slave you got no money of yer own! I truly do admire yer spunk but . . ."

The penitent responded easily, "The man who taught me about Yeshua, the Son of the God of Israel, held onto the stolen money I turned over to him. When I told him I needed to return to Colossae, he handed me the bag and told me to use what I must to make the journey. Then he wrote a letter to my master asking him to accept me back into his household and promising to make up any difference in what I had used and what I had taken. He will be following me to Ephesus shortly and will visit my master at that time."

The Captain turned and walked away leaning on the ship's rail and turning again toward Onesimus. "You are more than welcome to sail with us and . . . say . . . if you would like, you can sail for free if you would like to crew for me!"

Onesimus couldn't hide the great smile that lit up his face as he considered the mighty changes God had worked in his life. He nodded agreement and the Captain took him to the crew's quarters. "I'll give you today since you've been traveling, but I expect you to report bright and early tomorrow morning for duty!"

How changed he was! How changed his life! Miracles abounded all around him, God making a way for him to clear his past without putting more debt on either himself or Paulus!

It was clear to him that this was exactly what God was calling him to do at this time. There might come a time when more was required of him, but for right now, he needed to set things right and make certain that Philemon knew what had happened and why.

He settled into his hammock, rocking gently with the motion of the waves against the dock and thinking about how he would approach Philemon. He was praying that God would open Philemon's heart to accept the apology Onesimus planned to offer him . . . and knowing he was subject to the ultimate punishment if his master refused his apology.

Knowing that tomorrow would bring a world of change to his status from passenger to crew member, Onesimus thought he should take the opportunity to catch a little extra sleep and soon his breathing deepened and turned to gentle snores. The ship, held securely to the dock by its lines, rocked in safety as Onesimus slept.

The next few days were filled with hauling cargo, learning how the pulleys worked to raise the larger crates onto the ship, working at whatever the Captain told him to do, and making certain that he got a chance to talk to his Lord every night.

As he lay in his hammock, he would rub his sore muscles and reflect on the day's events. He would consider where he might have done better and where he had done very well. He would thank God for His help in the good times and the bad and would talk to Him about whatever was on his mind until he dropped off the sweet edge into sleep.

At the end of the week, Onesimus was overjoyed to see the lines cast off and the sails fill with wind as the ship began the reverse trek of Onesimus earlier voyage.

Captain Alban had made it clear, though, that the voyage wouldn't be as complicated as the previous one. There would be no stop in Sicily and only a short one-day stop in Crete. Then a quick sail to Ephesus and Onesimus would be almost... home. It seemed a little strange to Onesimus, but he was already thinking of the slaves' quarters in Colossae as home. The longing to be there again almost overwhelmed the last of his trepidation at the coming reunion with Philemon.

Most of that long voyage from Puteoli to Crete was filled with days of hard work and learning. At first, because of Onesimus's inexperience, much of that work took on the consistency of cabin boy duties, but because the captain liked Onesimus, it wasn't long before he was allowing the prodigal to take on the responsibilities of a seasoned sailor as well as letting him help sort out the ship's books. That task was made easier after Onesimus introduced Philemon's simple bookkeeping system to the ship's master and Alban, in turn, learned the method quickly and was quite happy with its simplicity.

Soon Onesimus found himself helping hoist the sails and securing the cargo, climbing the rigging for a turn at lookout and even standing on the cabin roof at the stern of the ship. He had been on the cabin roof about three times, watching the steersman and learning how to control the rudders. On his fourth turn, the Captain appeared on the deck below and bellowed, "Ignatius! Come on down here and help me out! Leave Onesimus to act as steersman for a short time!"

Ignatius stepped aside and let Onesimus take the rudder. Then, amid the runaway's protests that he wasn't ready, he jumped down to the Ship's Master while calling out, "You'll do fine! Just hold her steady, she'll take the course!" Then he was gone and Onesimus truly felt as if he were left holding the bag.

Lasea, the Cretian port, seemed to welcome the Swan with open arms and Onesimus was glad to be back on this peaceful island if only for a short time. This trip, the Swan was taking on a few crates of goods, some amphorae filled with olive oil, and about fifty bales of wool.

"It's almost not worth the time spent to stop," Captain Alban confided to Onesimus, "but it gives you boys a chance to go ashore for an hour or so after the loading is complete ... if you hurry!"

Onesimus tried to hide his grin as he nodded sagely. He knew as well as the captain did that really he was insuring the boat would be loaded by the time the tide went out. Even so, the crew set to with a will. They toted, hauled, and secured cargo until the job was done and there *was* enough time for the sailors to walk up the streets and locate whatever it was each of them wished for most on that long, hard voyage. For some, it was a hot meal served by a pretty girl. For others, it was just the pretty girl. It *could* be a clandestine visit to a flower seller just to savor the scents of beauty. Still others just wanted to walk on a surface that wasn't rocking beneath their feet. For Onesimus, the wish was to visit again that taverna where he'd met the traveler who told him about the ship from Adramyttium. He didn't believe he would meet up with the man again... but nevertheless, he wanted to revisit that place where he first heard the story of the man who defied a viper and who had lived to introduce Onesimus to the only One who could change any life offered up to Him in humility.

After a short visit with the owner and a glass of wine, Onesimus hurried back to the quay to find the Swan ready to cast off at the proper time. He reported to the captain and took up his station at the bow, watching carefully for hazards that might pose a threat to a ship under sail.

The voyage from Crete to Ephesus could take as little as three days. It could also take as much as a week or, if it met a fierce storm, two weeks or more.

For the first day and a half of this voyage the wind was slightly abaft of the beam and the ship scudded along at top speeds. Then the wind swung slightly to port and the voyage slowed, but it still wasn't necessary to tack to make forward movement. While Onesimus was eager to reach Ephesus and begin the last leg of his long journey, he found no reason to complain about the slower pace. And when, after five days, the Swan made port at Ephesus, Onesimus was somewhat reluctant to leave the ship and say his farewells to Captain Alban and his fellow crewmembers. He had learned a lot and had enjoyed his time as a crewman aboard the Swan.

He gathered his few belongings and had started to walk toward the captain when Alban hurried across the deck with his arms outstretched. "Onesimus, I tell you I have never been as impressed with a young man's eagerness to learn and work as I have been with you. When I made that offer to you so long ago, I was right to do so. I know you have something you feel you need to do, but remember my offer. If you come to the place where you can redeem yourself come back here to the port and watch for me. You will be more than welcome on my crew at any time!" he said sincerely.

Onesimus, from the depths of an enveloping hug, nodded his head and promised in a shoulder-muffled voice that he would do exactly as Alban instructed. As he pulled away Onesimus felt the Captain pushing something into his hand, "Not what your work was worth," he said gruffly, "but a little something to help you out. Not your master's money; this is but yours alone. You earned it."

Onesimus glanced down at his hand and saw there 15 denarii. It wasn't a grand amount, but with care he wouldn't have to borrow from the master's money any more. He rejoiced at the thought of not needing to indebt himself or Paulus any deeper.

He made his way onto the pier and moved off toward the port city. As he passed down the street he couldn't avoid the sight of the magnificent marble Temple to Artemis that stood next to the street. Made entirely of marble, the temple was an imposing sight. Its thirty-six tall columns and four statues of the Amazon women who were said to have founded the city outshined most of the beautiful things of the known world. The sun shining on the marble set the pillars and statues glittering as if sprinkled with gold.

He stopped and gazed at the shining marble walls, watching the worshipers coming and going with their hopes and dreams and wondered if they would ever find the truth of the one true God. He saw the temple prostitutes, dressed in gauzy see-through clothing (if they were dressed at all) plying their trade and playing the role they had been chosen to play by the priests of the goddess they served. His heart broke as he watched the sadness etched in almost every face and he closed his eyes and said a quick prayer that this temple of sorrow would soon crumble to dust and those who were bound by tradition, hope or lies to the false goddess would find freedom through the preaching of Paulus and others who would come to the city.

CHAPTER
TWENTY-SIX

Onesimus moved through the city and into the surrounding countryside quickly. He had a six-day journey ahead of him and was eager to complete it. Besides wishing to reach his final goal and face whatever punishment would be meted out to him as quickly as possible, he also remembered the fine young couple who had fed and housed him overnight and had refused any sort of recompense for it. He remembered Kiffien's good humor and Faith's tender prayer for his safekeeping. He wanted to stop at their home and let them know he had found the Way, as Faith had prayed, and to set his paths straight with them as well.

In the marketplace he had taken the time to make a small purchase and then had wrapped it in a veil he had also purchased. He was eager to see her face when Faith opened her little gift.

Up toward the surrounding countryside Onesimus walked, smiling and greeting fellow-travelers, realizing how much easier it was to travel when you were traveling openly and not having to hide in the sparse brush along the way. This time, as he walked he could smell the flowers of high summer; the honey lily, star of Bethlehem, columbine and gladiolus. All gave their fragrances to the air, making the short walk to Kiffien's house joyful as well as interesting. He could glance up and see the azure vault above and watch all types of birds, from finches to hawks, sailing on the sea of the heavens as easily as the Swan had sailed the Great Sea below. He was only about a half-league distance from the city when he came to the small but neat home of his previous benefactors. He stepped off the roadway and called out, "Kiffien, Faith! I have returned. Are you here?"

Faith appeared in the doorway. Her mouth turned up in a great smile as she hurried across the yard and put her hands on his shoulders.

"Zacheus! It is good to see you. Kiffien and I have been praying for you ever since you left and he will be so happy to see you again."

Onesimus shook his head and said, "I have much to tell you both, is he here?"

"He is away for a short time but he will be back for his supper," she laughed. "You know he would *never* miss a meal!"

Onesimus laughed. "I remember. Well, my story will wait until he gets here but I have something for you that just will *not* wait." With that, he pulled the little cloth-wrapped gift from his girdle and handed it to her.

"A gift?" she asked excitedly. "You really shouldn't have spent your money on me!"

"Considering that you gave me shelter and food, I wanted to get something for you. It isn't an important thing, but I hope you like it. Please open it."

Carefully, Faith unwrapped the small package. She gasped with pleasure when she saw the small mirror it held. Made of brass, the mirror shined in the sunlight. Its tortoise-shell handle was just the right size for a womanly hand and Faith had never seen such a beautifully carved frame.

"Thank you so much!" Faith said quietly. "I don't think I've ever seen such a beautiful and clear mirror. I will use it every day and think of you every time I do."

"Use what?" came Kiffien's familiar voice. "Think of someone else, will you? What will you use every day and think of someone else?" The laughter in his voice gave away the fact that he already knew who their visitor was. "Zacheus! It is good to see you again, my friend!"

"Before we go any further, talking about my adventures, I have a story to tell you that I hope you can accept," Onesimus said as he followed his hosts into their home.

Faith started bustling around, setting out barley cakes, eggs, and asparagus for supper but Kiffien, understanding that Onesimus had become very sober, took her hand and guided her to her seat at the table so they could listen together to what Onesimus had to say.

"First, I must tell you that my name is not Zacheus. I am Onesimus, a runaway slave," Faith gasped and Kiffien frowned. "I was running from my master when we met and I lied to you to protect myself from his wrath. Much has changed since last we were together and I would like to tell you about that right now. But, I must ask you to not form any opinions about me until I am done with my tale. I promise that, unlike the last time we talked, everything I will tell you will be the truth of the God you serve."

A span of silence was followed by Kiffien's nod and Onesimus continued, "My father sold me into slavery to pay some debts and a man name Philemon bought me . . .."

Faith and Kiffien listened intently as Onesimus recounted everything he had done and everything that had been done to him between that awful night in his father's garden and the night of his conversion.

"Paulus and I had a deep talk that night and when he again suggested that I needed to decide which God I would follow, I yielded to the Truth and became a disciple of Paulus and a worshiper of the Christ. I've spent the last two years, learning at the feet of Paulus as he awaited his trial before Caesar. And now, I am returning to my master to make straight my paths with those I lied to before. Please, forgive me for my perfidy, my brother and sister." Overcome with emotion, Faith reverted to what she knew best. She stood and finished laying the table for supper while Kiffien sat back in his chair and raised his hands above his head. "Praise be to God the Father and to His Son and to the Holy Ghost for answering our daily prayers!" he shouted. "Some adventure you have had, my brother! I suggest we move on from here and have some of Faith's wonderful barley cakes and eggs and . . . maybe a little cheese with it, Faith? Have we any cheese?"

Kiffien was gratified to see Faith turn from her storage area with a large piece of cheese in her hands. "Husband! Would I ever allow us to run out of cheese?"

After the meal was over, the three friends moved out of the house in search of a breeze. They seated themselves on rocks scattered around the front garden and talked quietly as they watched a couple of chickens pursue the same bug and laughed as the cockerel ran in front of them and scooped up the bug for himself. The indignation of the hens was plain to be seen.

"Poor little hens! That mean old man just snatches hope from you doesn't he?" Faith cried in feigned pity.

The men laughed and Kiffien asked, "Why don't you go help them gather bugs, Faith! You know how sorry you feel for them."

"UGH!" Faith replied with a shudder. "I have trouble chasing down a spider inside the house let alone chasing beetles for chickens!"

After a little more time, Kiffien addressed Onesimus, "I'm supposing you're going to want to be on the road early tomorrow."

"Yes. I've still a long walk ahead of me and the sooner I start the sooner I will finish."

Kiffien glanced over at Faith, and Faith, after glancing at the ground for a moment, looked up with a nod and smiled.

Jumping up, Kiffien grabbed Onesimus by the upper arm and said, "Come with me. I've something to show you."

He led his friend around the little house to a fenced area that contained a couple of goats and a couple of sheep. As they approached the fence, a small brown and white donkey ambled over and nudged Kiffien's hand, looking for a treat.

Onesimus watched as Kiffien dug a few chickpeas out of his pocket and held them out in his flattened hand to the little jenny.

"Her name is Lily," he explained. "Last year, we went to Laodicea to my cousin's wedding and my cousin told me to take Lily to ease our road home. He said we could return her the next time we came for a visit. You could do me a great service if you would deliver her to her owner as you pass through the city."

"That is very generous of you," Onesimus said with emotion. "It will certainly be easier to ride this little girl than it would be to walk the distance! Thank you."

"You are doing us a favor, friend. Lily has been with us almost a full year now and we've been wondering how we were going to get the time to take her back. Now both you and I are in better shape than we were yesterday!"

After a little more chatting Onesimus and his friends retired into the house where they settled down for the night in anticipation of an early rising.

What a wonderful day to begin a journey! Onesimus thought as he opened his eyes to a sunny day. The sky was blue with a few small, white clouds skimming along before the breeze.

A clatter from the other end of the house informed him that it wouldn't be long before he would be breaking his fast and then he realized how hungry he really was.

"Warm oaten cakes for breaking fast today," Kiffien said. "Faith got up extra early to make certain we had a nice warm meal before you leave and enough left over for you to carry some with you. That's why I love her!"

"I can see why," Onesimus replied as he made his way to the table. "If she were free, I'd offer her my hand and I've no doubt I could do better by her than you. After all, what is more secure than a position within slavery?"

He and Kiffien both laughed as Faith joined them at the table with fresh milk from the nanny and figs from their own tree. "Well, I'm just glad I'm already claimed!" she murmured quietly with a smile.

"May I?" Onesimus asked as he reached for the hands of his friends. At Kiffien's nod, he began, "Our Lord and Creator, how can we express our gratitude for all your blessings? For those who care for and help us we thank you. For sunny, breezy days we thank you. For oat cakes and nanny's milk we thank you. Bless our ways and bring us safely together again as your will commends. In the name of Christ Jesus our Savior, Amen."

Cakes and figs were selected and milk was poured before anything else was said.

"I'm planning on staying on this road right into Laodicea. I didn't have a mount last time. Could you tell me about how long it will take on Lily?" Onesimus asked.

Kiffien glanced at the table with a small, thoughtful frown between his eyebrows. "I believe it was almost as long as walking . . . about four-and-a-half or five days. But it's much pleasanter when you can ride. I will give you directions to my cousin's house before you leave and I know he would be more than happy to let you stay there a night before you finish your journey."

CHAPTER TWENTY-SEVEN

While it was true that riding a donkey was a lot easier on the legs than walking, Onesimus reflected, it was a lot harder on other parts of the anatomy. Donkeys were much bonier along the spine than horses and sometimes that prominence became annoyingly noticeable. He shook his head at his own moaning and slipped from the donkey's back to the ground. A little walk would do him good.

The village where the slave had been caught and branded loomed in the near distance and he slipped his hand inside his cloak to feel the coins he held separate there from Philemon's purse. This was money he had earned. He wanted to spend a couple denarii on some cheese and maybe a couple of roasted eggs for his dinner. He still had one of Faith's oaten cakes. It was still edible, though a little dry around the edges. He had husbanded his money carefully and had bought nothing that wasn't necessary (except the mirror and veil, he amended) so he had enough to feed himself quite well for the rest of the trip.

There before him stood the merchant's shop near the corner where Onesimus could still hear the screams of the runaway. He entered and haggled his way into two eggs and a wedge of strong goat cheese. As he was turning to leave another man came in the door.

"Ave, Augurius!" he called in good humor. "Have you heard the latest news of that moon-mad cult near Colossae? Their leader, Philemon, has truly gone to graze with his sheep! I hear he is commanding all his slaves to make sacrifice to this Yeshua he worships!"

Augurius shook his head. "What have we to do with a foreign god?!? Haven't we got enough gods of our own? I heard he lost one of his slaves a couple of years ago because the slave refused to eat roasted babies!"

"Now, that I would never doubt!" his companion replied. "I know he lost at least one as a runaway a couple of years ago and he is still searching for him when he can get away. They say his plans for him are not to welcome him back with open arms! I've heard he's beaten a couple of his slaves almost to death for refusing to worship this foreign god of his."

"Well, I certainly wouldn't want to be that slave if Philemon finds him!" Augurius declared.

Onesimus walked on, listening to them cluck and tsk like two old women over the antics of the "moon mad" Philemon.

At first, it was easy to dismiss the gossip as just that... gossip. But as he walked, and then rode, and then walked some more, the fear began to grow within his breast.

What if what they had said was true? Onesimus thought. After all, wasn't Philemon's own father moon struck? Am I really ready to walk on directly into the arms of a madman? And one who was by all I've heard, as mad as a March hare?

He shook his head, frowning in concentration. That was crazy! *The very thought of Philemon beating slaves and forcing them to worship Yeshua is completely contrary to everything I've learned about Philemon and his–our–God!*

Still, he rode on. The fear was with him, but so was a calm assurance that God held his life in His hands and would let nothing happen to Onesimus that wasn't for His good and the good of the Kingdom. He traveled another two or three leagues before he decided it was time to stop for the night. By this time, his fear had settled into a vague unease. Yet the peace had not–could not–leave him.

Slipping from the donkey's back, he led her off the road to a sheltering oak where he tied her. He drew the eggs and cheese from his girdle and settled down beside the donkey to eat and then to sleep until time to move on. Because it was high summer, there seemed to be no urgent need for a fire, so he decided to forego that particular comfort. He was, after all, just a day's distance from Laodicea and perhaps one and a half days' journey after that to Colossae.

The pilgrimage had been tiring and Onesimus slept deeply and dreamlessly until the little Jenny stirred and bumped into him. He awoke with a start, but began to settle back into sleep, when he heard the noise that had disturbed his companion.

A strange snuffling, snorting noise was coming from the other side of the tree. Half asleep, he couldn't place it at first. He listened and the noises continued for several minutes. Then the snorting changed to a high-pitched squealing that instantly revealed its origin to Onesimus.

It was a wild boar searching out acorns and, perhaps, mushrooms in the midnight darkness.

A picture flashed into his mind. He had seen many of those boars as a boy, hunting them with his father. Boar hunting wasn't for the timid, his father used to say. Hunting boar was like hunting bear or wolves . . . boars were dangerous. Covered in coarse, dark hair, boars knew exactly how to use their long, curving tusks to protect their territory and kill any predators . . . including men who drew attention to themselves.

The snuffling started up again and began to move closer to where the donkey and the man lay together. Onesimus thought hard, wishing he had built a fire, hoping to remember a long-forgotten weapon he could use, anything to defend himself and the little Jenny but there was nothing. Finally, he resorted to the thing he knew he should have done *first*. He began to pray. Quietly . . . *very* quietly.

When the quiet praying became quiet praising, as it usually did with Onesimus, the boar gave one more loud *snort!* and headed away from the little camp, back into the thicket.

Onesimus once more slept and the donkey, perhaps sensing the spirit of this kindly man, laid her head on his chest and drifted off as well.

CHAPTER TWENTY-EIGHT

Onesimus stood in the olive grove watching the house and grounds of Philemon. He patted his girdle, making certain the all-important letter from Paulus was still with him. Without that letter, Onesimus doubted if he could ever convince his master that he had changed. Without that letter, it was possible that Philemon would have him beaten or even killed for what he had done and no one would care . . . except Paulus when he arrived.

Of course, Philemon might have him beaten or killed even with the letter, but Onesimus felt it was much less likely. He decided he would pray one last time before approaching the house. So he knelt right where he was and began to pray, "Father, I know I am not worthy of all the grace and mercy you have shown me and I thank you for everything I have learned about you. I kneel before you in humility and ask only that you give me the courage to face whatever is in store for me. Grant that I will acquit myself with humility and obedience and let me not try to defend myself with argument but rather help me to accept whatever fate Philemon decides for me. In the name of Christ, Amen."

It was the midday. Everyone should be at the midday meal right now.

He stepped out of the olive grove and into the meadow that surrounded the house. Strangely, it felt as if he were coming home.

He pulled the letter from his sash and walked up on the porch. He was just about to call out when a shout came from inside. Someone had spotted him.

"Onesimus! It's Onesimus! He's come back!" Petros, a full foot taller than when Onesimus ran, jumped toward the door his now cracking voice calling, "Father! Onesimus is . . ."

Philemon appeared behind the boy and crossed rapidly toward the door. Onesimus almost took to his heels as he saw his former master bearing down on him, but he stood his ground even when Philemon reached roughly for him. The all-engulfing hug his master bestowed upon him was not what he had expected at all but it didn't take long for him to return the hug.

Philemon pulled away and the runaway was startled to see tears in the man's eyes. "Onesimus, my son! For so long we have watched for you. I have much to tell you and," he dropped his eyes to his feet and then looked up again, "an apology to give you! Do you remember that just before you... left . . . Petros came in and insisted that I go with him to his grandfather's cottage that he had something to show me?"

Onesimus thought back to that day and then nodded. He and Philemon found seats on the portico.

"It was with great joy that I returned to the press room after that little trek. I was ready to tell you that all was well. Petros had found out that his grandfather, struck by the moon as he was, had taken the two missing amphorae of oil from one of the wagons because he felt he would need that much to bathe in so that he could slip from the grasp of the Angel of Death! And then we found you gone." This last was said quietly with great sorrow.

"I am so sorry I accused you, Onesimus and I am sorry that I was not a better Christian in your presence. Even being with me every day for four months you were afraid for your life! No slave should ever have to fear for their lives when their master is a follower of Christ!"

Philemon fell silent and Onesimus swallowed a large lump that had grown in his throat.

"I, too, have an apology, Master. I should never have assumed the worst of you. I knew you were a kind and just man and I did you a grave injustice when I stole your money and ran away. My sorrow for what I have done to you is unbearable and how I have ruined my own reputation would be agonizing except that I can see, in all of this, the very hand of Yahweh at work in my life."

Philemon raised startled eyes to Onesimus and tipped his head to the left.

"Your life and teachings did much to help me understand your religion, but while I was on my . . . flight . . . I met a man who slowly introduced me personally to the God of Israel. I stayed with him and learned from him for many months, knowing from the first that I would need to come back and make things right with you. At long last, he gave me a letter to give to you and told me to tell you he has plans to come to you shortly. Here it is!" He handed the letter over to Philemon and smiled when his master saw from whom the letter came.

"Paulus? You lived with Paulus and learned from him? How wonderful!" He exclaimed. "And he is coming here? Do you know when? How is he? Is he well? We heard that he was under house arrest for a while. Can you . . ."

Onesimus smiled and answered all the questions he could about Paulus's state of health and all he knew about Paulus's plans to visit Colossae until finally, everything seemed to have been said. They had talked through the afternoon and the sun was heading toward its bed. The mourning doves were roosting in the nearby trees as their quiet cooing uttered peace to the weary soul.

"Father," Blandina called from inside the house. "Supper is almost ready."

"Oh! My! It's late, Onesimus! And no work has been done this livelong day," Philemon finally said. "Too late to start clerking for me right now, so why don't you go back to the slaves' quarters and tell them I want you to settle in? Supper will be served there shortly and I'm sure they've heard that you're back with us. Justin will have made arrangements for you and . . . I expect to see you bright and early tomorrow. We have much to do to prepare for the harvest!"

"Yes, sir! Bright and early!" Onesimus replied. "Bright and early!"

Aω

AUTHOR BIO

J OYCE FOX was born in Lansing, Michigan one cold February midnight, the sister to four elder siblings. As the youngest child she grew to learn to "hang tough" during the rocky times of life. People sometimes see her as aggressive and outspoken but she uses those characteristics to speak up for those who have no voice. This tenacity of will, her love for words, and her hope in Jesus brought her to the news industry. It's also helped keep her marriage to her beloved ministerial husband alive for more than 44 years. Joyce is retired from TriStates Public Radio WIUM/WIUW of Macomb, Illinois and has spent many years working as a volunteer with the Salvation Army. Joyce now resides in Cleveland, TN. where she is currently studying for licensure in Clinical Mental Health at the Pentecostal Theological Seminary.

www.ingramcontent.com/pod-product-compliance
Lightning Source LLC
Chambersburg PA
CBHW030514020726
47494CB00004B/1095